THE 'BAGO BLUES

John O'Neill

ISBN: 0692064095
ISBN 13: 9780692064092
Library of Congress Control Number: 2018901788
John O'Neill Books, Bethesda, MD

Novels by John O'Neill

Baby Girl Lauren
Blue Death

For my mother and all of her wonderful friends

ONE

Do not go gentle into that good night but rage, rage against the dying of the light.

Dylan Thomas

MO

I n a few short minutes, the broad shadows cast from the back of the Westwood Retirement Home softened and merged into the settling dusk. A light blinked on in an upstairs room, and then another down the hall. A few more minutes passed, and, with the dusk deepening, Val could now see through the large rectangular window of the first-floor nursing station. A tall figure dressed in white, probably Velma, was standing in front of a counter, and a shorter figure whom Val did not recognize was talking on a telephone. Val glanced at her watch—five more minutes.

Her cell phone rang. Sophie.

"The goddamn window won't open," she said.

"It's the humidity. You have to hit it hard. With your palm. You know what I mean, don't you?"

"Of course I know what you mean. I'm not a damn idiot. What, you think I never had any windows?"

"I didn't—"

"I tried hitting it. But if I hit it too hard, they'll think I'm banging for them. I told them I was tired and going to bed. I'm sick and tired of this whole damn place is what I am."

"Calm down, Sophie. Take one of those butter knives you keep in your nightstand and pry it open. I can't come over there yet. There's someone in the nursing station right by the window."

"Where are you?"

"In the parking lot. I can see your window."

"Well, you're going to have to help me get out, so you may as well get your fanny over here."

"It's still too light. Five more minutes."

"I might be dead in five minutes. I don't feel so hot."

"Then maybe you shouldn't go tonight. Mo will understand."

"No way. I'm getting out of here one way or another."

"Okay. Well, just see if you can get the window open. Did you lock your door?"

"No, that would really set them off. I fixed my bed, though. Nice and fat—just like me."

"Good. I'll be there in five minutes."

Val could still see Velma in the nursing station. Tired from the trip to the hospital the night before to see Mo, and a restless sleep after that, she put her head back and closed her eyes. Even though it was still August, she sat in her car with the engine off and the windows open, the outside air moist and heavy and clinging to her face and neck in a sticky film. She was not particularly comfortable, but with September just a few days away, and the evenings slowly dying, she knew the air would soon begin to cool. She took a deep breath and let it out through her nose. Yes, slight as it was, it was there—a hint of a breeze carrying the barest trace of cooling air, of waning summer. A raft of air lifting her, carrying her back, carrying her away.

In a moment she was at the beach, late into an August evening, Jules next to her in a chair by the ocean. His eyes were closed, his face expressionless, his tanned scalp and face golden in the setting sun. She wanted to touch him, but she knew he would not come to her here. Only deep into the night would he come alive, his eyes smiling at her, playing with her. She let him go and turned to the low, rolling waves of the evening ocean curling down the beach. They broke softly onto the sand, almost silently, gliding effortlessly toward her chair. At her feet they would pause for a poignant moment, beckoning her to the water, beckoning her to join them as the mother force gently sucked them back.

For a few seconds—and she didn't quite know why—she saw Henry. Henry, young and serious, bent in their little garden as if the plants he tended were the children he desired. They'd had Bill, an accident. Then, just as her love had faded, so did he, as if he were, after all, just a brief ten-year prelude. A brief prelude to Jules and their life together. That's all ten years were anyway. A nothing, a blip in time. Even now, close to her eighty-second birthday and with a memory that still served her quite well, she often had to think hard about what Henry looked like when she'd married him and even harder about when she'd left him.

Her phone rang again.

"Come on, Val. What are you waiting for? I'm thirsty."

Val straightened and peered through the windshield at the nursing-station window. "I'll be right there. I think Velma's leaving."

She got out and made her way across the parking lot staying between the cars and the wing of the building that housed the Westwood nursing station. When she reached the courtyard outside Sophie's ground-floor window, she moved behind the large central oak. Stepping gingerly through the mulched flowerbed, she squeezed through two ligustrums and reached Sophie's window where she heard something rubbing hard against the wooden frame. Sophie had the curtains pulled aside, and she pointed up with her thumb. Val nodded, and they both pushed up on the frame at the same time. The window squeaked and moved an inch or two. They pushed again and moved it a foot. Another push and it was open enough for Sophie to get her head and shoulders out.

"I can do this," she said, looking from the windowsill to the flowerbed. She ran her hand over the sill. "No problem."

"Are you sure? I can go by myself tonight. Mo's not expecting to see you."

"I told you—no way."

Val pushed the window up a few more inches, and they looked at each other.

"Now what, Miss Smarty Pants?"

Val looked from the windowsill to the ground and back to Sophie. "Umm, I'm not sure headfirst is such a good idea."

"No shit, Sherlock. Here goes," Sophie said. She lifted her leg a foot off the floor and stopped. She looked at the floor, the window. "My damn skirt's too tight. It's the food in here, I'm telling you."

"Maybe you need your desk chair."

"Maybe a crane is what I need." Sophie dragged her wooden desk chair over to the window and managed to get up on it on her knees. She hiked her skirt up her thighs, and then, with Val holding her arm through the window, she slowly lifted her leg again. Well short of the windowsill, she had to stop. "Got any more bright ideas," she said, putting her leg back down.

Val put her head through the window and looked around. "Yeah. Push your desk over a couple of feet so that you can sit on the edge, and then I can help you get your legs out."

Sophie climbed down, pushed her desk a few feet with her hips, climbed back up on her chair, and then managed to get up onto the desk. "Here goes nothing," she said between breaths and lifted her leg with Val's hands on either side of her. A lavender sandal and a speckled bare calf came out first. Her skirt was now pushed up further around her hips, exposing her pale, fleshy thighs and white Hanes cotton underpants. "Reminds me of when I was sixteen," she said, inching her torso up onto the sill and then her other leg. "I got pretty damn good at this."

"You haven't lost a thing," Val said, now with a hand on each of Sophie's legs. "Not one bit. Careful now. No emergency rooms tonight."

"Oh, I can still get around," Sophie said with a grunt. "Don't you doubt that for one minute."

"I know. That's why you have a curfew."

"Funny. Very funny. I told you, Val," she said, her breaths heavier, "don't get me started. I'm serious, too. I don't feel so hot."

"You shouldn't be doing this then. I'll go see Mo."

"And let you get all the credit? No way."

"Sophie, if you're sick, you're sick. I'll tell her you were halfway out the window."

"I didn't say I was sick. I said I wasn't feeling so hot. Damn. They don't make windows like they used to. I swear to God, they used to be bigger." Sophie's legs were out and spread-eagled, and her skirt stuck on the sill beneath her. "Maybe you should pull a little."

"Okay, but keep holding on, so you don't fall out." Val stood between Sophie's legs and put an arm around each of her thighs. At first she gently pulled backward, which moved nothing.

"Come on, Val, pull," Sophie said, her breaths getting faster and heavier.

Val pulled harder, and Sophie's hips moved through the sill.

"You okay over there? Do you need some help?" It was a man's voice. A voice that sounded as if help was coming whether it was needed or not.

"No thanks, we're fine," Val called over her shoulder. "We're just working on a planter."

"'A planter?'" Sophie managed between breaths. "*Really.* Christ, that's that Charles guy. The Romeo. Christ almighty. What if he comes over here?"

"Are you sure? I'd be happy to help." The man had moved off the sidewalk and into the courtyard, his dog whining to get at them. Though she couldn't see him, Val could sense him peering through the bushes, the dog straining on the leash.

"We're fine. My husband's right inside. Thanks anyway."

"Oh. Okay."

Val didn't hear him move away, but she could tell Sophie was having trouble breathing. She pulled hard and then pulled hard again until Sophie's chest was through, and she had to let go of her legs. With Sophie's feet on the ground, she quickly took hold of her waist and tried to steady her. Sophie's head came free, and the sudden weight of them going backward took them both to the ground, Val on her back and Sophie on top of her, her skirt hiked up high on her waist, her legs jerking like a beetle tipped on its back.

For a moment they were quiet, assessing the damage. Then Val started to laugh, and Sophie, rolling off her, started a giggle of her own.

"Oh, my word," Val said.

"'Oh, my word,'" Sophie said, sitting up and catching her breath. "How about Christ Almighty? How about—"

"Shhh!" Val said, putting a hand over Sophie's mouth. "Let's stay here another minute or so. Let it get just a little darker."

Sophie rubbed her calf and bent over to peer at it. "Goddamn it, I'm going to have a bruise for a month. Now they'll think I can't walk without running into everything too."

Val sat up and leaned over to look at Sophie's leg. "I don't see any blood."

"Just wait. It'll look like a damn plum in about ten minutes. Come on, let's go—I need a drink. Romeo better be gone, or I'm going to give that little rat a good kick."

Val stood up, put out her hands, pulled Sophie to her feet. She closed the window, put an arm around Sophie's shoulder, and steered them toward her car. "You need to get a new doctor, you know. He's treating you like an imbecile. I mean, think about it.

Think about what you just actually did. You could have broken your hip or something."

"It's not him," Sophie said, her eyes glazing. "He's just a wimp. He just does whatever the gestapo wants."

Val squeezed her. "Sorry. We'll talk about it later."

They reached Val's Lexus, and Sophie wiped her eyes. "What'd you buy?" she asked. "Something good, I hope."

"Chalk Hill. Sixty bucks a bottle. I bought five."

Sophie gave Val a high five and smiled for the first time that night. "Good girl."

Val turned into the visitor's parking lot at St. Joseph's Hospital.

"Northwest isn't good enough for her," Sophie said, just as she always did when they visited Mo. According to Sophie, there were two perfectly good hospitals between Mo's house and St. Joseph's, which indeed there were. "Make us drive halfway across the damn city. It's not like they got a lock on heaven, you know. As a matter of fact, most of the ones I know—"

"Don't start with that now, Sophie. You know she's sick."

Sophie, rummaging through a side pocket in Val's purse, didn't respond.

"Are you sure that's a good idea?" Val asked.

"I just want a half," Sophie said. "I told you twice now—I don't feel so hot."

Val was silent for a moment. "You know it makes you cuckoo when you take that and you drink. Maybe even a half isn't such a great idea."

Sophie found the bottle of Xanax, took out a tablet, broke it in half, swallowed it dry, and shrugged. "I'm not driving. Look," she said, holding up the bottle. "It says right here, 'Do not drive a motor vehicle when taking this medicine.' Looks like you're the DD."

Val shook her head but didn't respond.

Sophie was still holding the plastic bottle up to the light. "Oh, shit, I can't operate heavy machinery either. I guess I'll use the little one tonight."

"Stop it," Val said, smiling. She parked and retrieved an over-sized handbag from the back seat. "Mo's not doing well."

"She tell you that?"

"No, I can tell. Besides, she was in here just last week."

Sophie didn't answer. Her mother and only sister had both died of breast cancer. They made their way across the parking lot, Val slowing to stay abreast of Sophie, who was limping slightly.

"Are you okay?" Val said. "Don't be a hero."

"I'm fine now. I wish I had broken my leg, though. Make 'em all look like idiots."

The double glass doors to the lobby of St. Joseph's Hospital slid open, and they went to the elevator without checking in at the front desk. Val pushed the button for the fifth floor, and they waited quietly, heads bent, hands folded in front of them. Val had ridden this elevator for the last four days and probably ten other days just in the last month. She glanced at Sophie, whose leg was indeed starting to turn purple, and the downward spiral of their card group in the last year settled on her heavily. When she'd first met Sophie who had moved down from New York to be closer to her daughter Roz, Sophie was living in her own apartment and driving on her own. Now she was in the Westwood Retirement Home on a curfew and with her car and driver's license confiscated by Roz. Mo had still been living in the house she and her late husband had lived in for forty-three years and had not been in a hospital for ten years. Now she was living with her daughter Mary Catherine and seemed to be in St. Joseph's every month. Lily's mind was going by the day, and she was now in assisted living. Goldie was finally done with Frank's seven-year, money-draining death march and faced an uncertain future. And she herself? She kept herself so busy with doctor's appointments and hospital visits that she tried not to think about it.

The elevator doors opened. In the central area between the east and west wings of the oncology ward, they stopped and looked at the numbers on the wall. "Hold on," Val said. "They changed her room today. Mary Catherine has been bugging the nurses all week about the other lady in her room. She's Chinese, and half of Chinatown must have been in there." She looked at a note in her phone. "East, five five three four."

Walking purposefully down the hall, they looked straight ahead as if they knew exactly where they were going and why. Nosy nurses had a particular affinity for anyone who looked confused, particularly anyone over the age of sixty-five. Tonight they were lucky. The halls were quiet, and room 5534 was only four doors down from the elevators. Val checked the door just to be sure— Maureen Flanagan. And there was no other name on the door— Mary Catherine had won, which was particularly fortuitous. Val took Mo's clipboard off the railing outside the room and studied it for a moment. Then they slipped inside, pausing to accommodate to the dimmer light and to make double sure they were not interrupting anything in the first bed. The first bed was indeed empty, the curtain between the two beds drawn.

They moved past the curtain and paused again, watching Mo in silence. Her eyes were closed, her breaths regular as if she were sleeping. Although the cancer that had started in her breast had spread to her lymph nodes and to at least one lumbar vertebra, she was not thinning in the normal way of those with a malignancy spiraling slowly out of control. She was headed in the other direction—bloated from the prednisone that controlled her arthritis and the unrelenting pain in her back. Her cheeks, full of the fair-skinned flush of the Irish, were unnaturally puffy, as were her eyelids and neck. The inner aspects of her arms were almost covered with large bruises from the incessant blood-letting, and the tops of her arms were mottled and bruised from the sun and the pred-nisone. Her hair was perfect—a reddish-brown wig that the five of them had picked out together.

Mo opened her eyes and smiled, a gesture reserved for friends and priests.

"Jesus, Mary, and Joseph," she said tartly. "Look what the cat drug in." She opened her arms for a hug from each of them. Then, lifting her head and looking around for intruders, she looked at Val. "I am dying for a glass of wine. Please tell me you brought some wine."

"Chalk Hill Chardonnay, 2014. What's your pleasure? Cup? IV? No NG tube, so that's out."

"Thank God. Let's start with a cup. These new IVs are hell to figure out." She handed Val her Styrofoam cup of ice chips. "Better put it in this. I hate to ruin good wine, but I got a real witch with me tonight. Chalk Hill. I don't think I've had that one before. I hope it wasn't expensive, Val."

"You bet it was," Sophie said proudly. "Sixty bucks a bottle. It's part of Val's plan."

"Part of what?" Mo said, lifting her head.

"Nothing," Val answered. "Tim and Mary Catherine already came tonight, didn't they?"

"And Paul and Margaret. I sent them home an hour ago."

"You're NPO, aren't you?"

"Yeah. Might get the tube in the morning. They think they see something in my intestine. God knows where. I stopped listening after a while."

"You sure you want to drink wine tonight?"

"Oh, my Lord, yes. You know if they say morning, it won't be until afternoon."

Val got up and moved a chair a few inches in front of the door. She took a soft cooler out of her bag, uncorked a bottle of Chalk Hill Chardonnay, and almost filled Mo's cup. Next she took two hospital cafeteria coffee cups and filled them halfway. The wine stashed back in her bag, she and Sophie moved to Mo's side.

"To Mo," Val said, extending her cup.

"To my friends," Mo said, touching her cup to theirs. She took a long drink, put her head back, sighed. "I didn't think you were coming. I was about to cry."

"Of course we were coming," Sophie said. "You should have seen me. I got out of that window like a sixteen-year-old in heat."

"She was something," Val said, shaking her head.

"Your window! Oh, my. Does that silly Dr. Crawford have you on a curfew?"

"Yeah. He didn't like my little walk down River Road."

"What *were* you doing anyway?" Val asked.

"Beats me," Sophie said. "He thinks one of those new medicines I'm on makes me loopy."

"She threw me under the bus, Mo. She told them I asked her out."

Sophie shrugged. "I thought you did ask me out. Who else would I have been out with at midnight?"

"Well, they're pretty much right about the medicines, particularly with you-know-what, Miss Cuckoo Bird. I told you what happens when you drink and take that."

Sophie rolled her eyes at Mo. "I got another Roz here, Mo."

"So when do you think you can go home?" Val said abruptly. "You need to be out of here by Friday."

"Why? What's today anyway?"

"It's Wednesday. Frank died yesterday. His service is Friday."

Mo's eyes instantly moistened. "Oh, I'm so sorry for Goldie. Is she okay?"

"He was comatose, Mo," Val said. "She wanted him to die."

"Oh no, she didn't. Don't say that, Val. Nobody *wants* their husband to die. Oh, poor Goldie."

Val raised her brow and looked at Sophie. Sophie shook her head slightly, but Val ignored her. "Mo," Val said, "she doesn't have any money left. It was costing her almost a thousand dollars a day."

"She still loved him, Val," Mo said. "He was her husband. Geez, of all people you should understand that."

"I understand she used to cry every day."

"Okay, Val, enough," Sophie said. "We got it. You think you'll be out by then, Mo? We'll come pick you up."

"My word, I certainly hope so. I'll tell Dr. O'Connor I have to go to a funeral." She was quiet for a moment. "What about the wake? If his funeral's Friday, it—"

Val was shaking her head. "There's no wake, Mo. All his friends are dead. Besides, Jews don't have wakes. They have shiva. The funeral service is Friday at Har Shalom."

Mo was quiet again. "Where's Lily?" she finally asked. "How is she?"

"She's in her room," Val answered, studying her cup.

"You think *I'm* in jail," Sophie said. "She can't even pee without someone following her around."

"Did she get in more trouble?" Mo asked.

"Depends who you ask," Sophie said sharply. "I think she's fine. Julie thinks she needs to be on an Alzheimer's ward."

"Oh my." Mo closed her eyes for a moment and then opened them and extended her cup. "Fill 'er up please," she said brightly. "You bring any cards?"

"I forgot," Val said, taking her cup. "Sorry. I'll remember tomorrow. You need some more ice chips in case the nurse comes in." Val went out to the kitchen and helped herself to ice chips. Back in the room, she placed the chair behind the door again and poured more wine. As she was putting the bottle away, the door opened and banged hard into the chair. The chair knocked again, quickly followed by the curtain being pulled back. A short, plump nurse with tiny drops of sweat beading on her forehead and upper lip stepped into view. She stopped and put her hands on her hips when she saw Val and Sophie and then moved to the foot of Mo's bed.

"Do you know why that chair was behind the door, Mrs. Flanagan? I almost broke my hand."

"That's the way it was when we came in," Val said. "I almost broke my hand, too. I presumed you wanted it like that. I thought it was a little strange, actually."

Val and Sophie sat down and moved their cups into their laps, almost into their crotches, and casually held their hands over them. Mo had already moved her cup under the sheets and between her legs.

The nurse frowned and looked around as if something were wrong. For several seconds she seemed to sniff the air, but the faint smell of alcohol apparently did not fit with anything else she saw in the room. She moved to the side of the bed and looked at Mo.

"Have you been sucking on your ice chips, dear?"

"Yes, ma'am."

The nurse looked around. "Where's your cup?"

"It was leaking," Val said. "I went to get her another one in the kitchen, but there were some people in there. I'll get her one in just a minute."

"That would be great. She needs to stay hydrated." Turning to Mo, she said, "Which way would you like to turn, Mrs. Flanagan?"

Mo peered at the name tag pinned to the nurse's blouse. "For what, Nurse Simpson?"

"Respiratory therapy. I need to make you cough. Doctor's orders."

Mo coughed. "There you go. All done."

The nurse shook her head. "You're a funny one. How about toward me?"

Mo coughed louder. "Is that better? My back really hurts, Nurse Simpson."

"Which way would it hurt the least, Mrs. Flanagan?"

Mo looked at Val and rolled her eyes.

"Miss Simpson," Val said, "we only have a few more minutes before we have to go home. It's getting late for us. Would it be possible to do this just a little bit later?"

"Not really," said the nurse. "I'm very busy tonight. And I'm doing you a favor as it is. Visiting hours are over, and her children were already here. I'm only letting you stay 'cause I know Mrs. Flanagan's husband is deceased."

She looked back to Mo. "So which way do you think is best for you?"

Mo put her hand between her legs and started to turn toward the window. As she turned there was a sharp crack beneath the sheets. The nurse straightened immediately, fear in her eyes.

"What was that?" she asked tentatively, searching Mo's face for pain or some answer.

Mo's eyes were shut tight, her face stoic as the cold wine ran between her legs.

"Mrs. Flanagan? Are you okay? What was that?"

"Maybe it was her backbone," Sophie said. "You know she's got bad bones, don't you? Are you okay, Mo?"

Mo seemed to grin. "I think I just need a moment to rest," she said to the nurse. "Maybe you could come back in a little while."

"We'll make her cough—promise," Sophie said.

"Mrs. Flanagan, I'm worried about you." The nurse leaned over to peer even more closely at Mo's face, her chubby thighs pushing into the edge of the bed. Suddenly she frowned. Straightening, she looked down to her white pants and the new yellowish damp spot just above her knee. First she put a hand over her mouth. Then she slowly pulled back the sheet and blanket as if she were afraid of what she would find.

"Oh my God," she said, her eyes wide. "You did break your back." She stabbed at a button over the bed and spoke sharply into the intercom. "Call the surgery resident stat. I think Mrs. Flanagan fractured a vertebra, and she's incontinent. She's going to need a catheter, and she might need her back stabilized." She stared at the mattress for another second or two, sniffed, leaned down, sniffed again. Straightening, she hit the intercom again and said, "And someone come in here and help me out ASAP. She's going to need a UA and a culture. She's also got some kind of infection."

The nurse pulled the covers down totally over Mo's hips and stared at the large wet circle on the bottom sheet and the few drops of clear golden fluid still clinging to Mo's thigh.

"You poor thing. Your whole bladder must have emptied. Try and relax, honey. We'll have all the help we need in just a minute."

Val moved to Mo's side, across from Nurse Simpson, and bent over her so that their faces were almost touching. Stroking her cheek with one hand, she reached between Mo's thighs with her other hand and took hold of the cup.

Looking over to Sophie, she said, "Sophie, are you okay?"

Nurse Simpson turned toward Sophie, who had stood up and backed against the wall. While she was looking at Sophie, Val slipped out the fractured cup and moved it behind her back.

"No, I'm not okay," Sophie said. "Not unless you think watching Mo break her back is a good time."

"Why don't you sit down before you faint then," Val said with a little smile. Then turning back to Mo, "You look tired all of a sudden." She wiped a tear from Mo's cheek, leaned close to her again, and kissed her on the forehead. "Hang in there, girl. Everything will be okay." Straightening, she moved back to her chair, picked up her purse, took Sophie by the arm, headed out.

They were silent in the hall, in the elevator, in the lobby. Outside, Sophie said, "Now what? How long is that going to keep her in there?"

"God knows. We'll have to think of something. Goldie will understand, but I know she'd really like to see Mo there."

"Do you think she can do it?"

"How so?"

Sophie didn't answer right away. "I mean, what if they move her? What if we can't get to her? How long can she go?"

"You mean without wine?"

Sophie hesitated and then said, "Yeah, that's exactly what I mean."

"Good question," Val said. "To tell you the truth, I don't know."

⇥ ⇤

Sophie got out of the front seat and hit her right calf on the edge of the car door. "Christ, I'm going to look like a damn plum tree before the night's over."

"Slow down," Val said. "Let me help you. We gotta get you back through that window."

"No problem," Sophie said, closing the door with a sideways stutter step. With her hand still on the car, she steadied herself. "You get out, you get back in."

Val took hold of her arm. "Maybe that last glass of wine in the park wasn't such a good idea."

"I'm fine. Lighten up. You really are starting to sound like Roz."

"The day I sound like Roz you can get your own wine."

"Okay, I take it back. Damn it's dark out here."

They made it through the courtyard to the window and stopped. For a long moment, both of them just stood there and stared.

"Maybe this isn't going to be so easy," Sophie said. "I had the chair inside to get up on."

"Right. Hold on—I don't know why I didn't think of this before. I'll be right back. Don't go anywhere."

When Val returned from her car, she was holding a milk crate. "I had this in my trunk. You never know, do you?" She set the milk crate down, pushed the window up, stepped back, stared again. "Hmm. I think it's headfirst this time, dear. You can grab hold of the chair and ease yourself down." Val reached the window and pushed the desk back as far as she could. "Okay, dear. Here we go."

"Right-O." Sophie hiked up her skirt, stepped up on the milk crate, put her head and shoulders through the window, and took hold of the desk chair. Val lifted her legs up and was pushing her in when the little Yorkie started barking.

Yap, yap. Yap, yap, yap.

"Christ Almighty," she said, her head almost on the chair. "It's Romeo again. Get me through here—I can't breathe."

"Hold on." Val pushed, pushed again, and Sophie, still holding onto the chair, slid through with a thump.

Yap, yap, yap. "You sure you don't need help over there? You've been working on that planter for a long time."

"Hold on, I'll be right there," Val called over her shoulder.

Sophie rolled off the chair and stayed spread-eagled on the floor. "Does that little rat have its rabies vaccine?" she yelled when she had caught her breath.

"Shhh!" Val said. "You're supposed to be asleep. Are you okay?"

"I'm fine. I hate that little rat, though. The damn thing tried to bite me once."

"Go to bed. You have an appointment in the morning. I'll go take care of Romeo."

"Oh, you do that," Sophie said. "Take care of him good. Maybe he'll have a heart attack. Stupid dog."

SOPHIE

Dr. Andrew Crawford paused over Sophie's left calf to study the bruise that now looked as if a ripe eggplant had been stuffed under her skin. He made a little clucking noise and then another after studying the large flat bruise on her right calf that had several scratches coursing through it.

"Did you fall?"

"No, I did *not* fall. One of those good-for-nothing aides moved my desk chair and never bothered to tell me."

Dr. Crawford made another noise—something between a grunt of acknowledgment and a doubting snort—and took out a reflex hammer. With a quick flick of his wrist, he rapped the tendon over her right knee, watched her foot jerk out, made a note in her chart. Putting the hammer away, he said, "Those are pretty bad bruises, Sophie. Either you hit that chair pretty hard or you're not clotting properly."

Sophie rolled her eyes and looked away.

"You're going to need some clotting studies," he said.

"Oh, for God's sake, Andrew. I'm fine. Old people bruise."

"Not like that."

"It's that damn aspirin then. Why don't you take me off it? I'm not having any ministrokes or whatever you call them. I'm sick of looking like someone took a bat to me."

"Because you need them."

"For what? For who? So I can live to be ninety-three? I don't want to be ninety-three, Andrew. When are you and the gestapo going to understand that?"

"Okay. All done. You can get dressed, and let's talk in my office for a minute."

"What, you think I'm not serious?"

"Sophie, it's normal to get discouraged sometimes. The reality is you're in pretty good health and you're fortunate you have a family to help take care of you. I take care of a lot of lonely people who would love to have what you have. Go ahead and get dressed, and I'll be with you in a minute."

"The reality is, you're not eighty-three."

"I'll be there in a minute, Sophie."

"Yeah, right. Remember I got diabetes. I can't go an hour without eating. We already spent an hour with all the lunatics in the parking lot. You need to move, you know."

"In a minute, Sophie. Relax. It's not good for you."

Roz was sitting in Dr. Crawford's office, a legal-sized notebook in her lap and a pen in hand. Sophie's medical history, surgical history, medications, and all of her doctors' names and addresses were printed out in a neat document, which she was busily reviewing.

"What, they kicked you out of the waiting room?" Sophie said. "I told you this was *my* appointment."

"Dr. Crawford thought it would be best if I listened also."

"Oh, really? The two of you don't trust my memory now either. Well, let me—"

"Mom, I didn't say that. It's just better to have two sets of ears."

"You mean when you're senile." Sophie sighed and sat across from Dr. Crawford's desk. "I hope you brought lunch. It'll be a while."

"He's doing his best, Mom. You saw all the people in the waiting room. Did you show him your legs?"

"He's not blind, Roz. They're just bruises. If you want to do something, why don't you tell those good-for-nothing aides to stay out of my room?"

Dr. Crawford strode in ten minutes later and sat down. "Thanks for the update, Roz," he said, picking up the copy of Sophie's medical document that Roz had placed on his desk.

"I thought this was my appointment, Andrew?"

"Come on, Sophie. You know Roz is on top of all this." Then tapping the document with his pen: "Okay. Hypertension is stable, angina's stable, cholesterol's okay, arthritis is stable, and your renal function is adequate. All your medications in that regard are pretty much where we want them, so we can leave them alone. Now, here are the problems. Your glucose is still too high. Diet and exercise," he said, glancing at Sophie's midsection, "aren't cutting it. You may need an oral hypoglycemic soon and maybe even insulin. We're going to give it a few more weeks." He paused, this time looking more at Roz. "Wine has a lot of sugar in it. Are you drinking more than we talked about, Sophie? One glass a night is okay. That's it, though."

"I think she often has more than that," Roz said. "Particularly when she's out with her friends."

"I thought it was good for your heart," Sophie said. "Isn't that why the French live so long?"

"Not when you have diabetes and high blood pressure and high cholesterol," Dr. Crawford said.

Sophie sighed and looked out the window.

"Okay, we'll give it a few weeks, Sophie. Lighten up on the wine, though. Okay?"

Sophie looked back to him. "Yeah sure, Andrew. One glass a night."

Roz shot Sophie a look of irritation and shook her head.

"Now, as I was saying before, you might not be clotting properly. We'll need a CBC and maybe some clotting studies. You can do that on the way out. And lastly—"

"Hold on a sec," interrupted Roz, who was busily writing on her notepad. She looked up. "You lost me there. What do you mean she's not clotting properly? Is that what's the matter with her legs?"

Sophie shook her head and shot Dr. Crawford a nasty look. "It's nothing, Roz. I told you—they're just bruises."

"I think it's probably okay, Roz," Crawford said. "They're a little larger than most of the ones I see, but the aspirin will do that. Alcohol, too. Let's just make sure she's clotting normally." He paused and took off his glasses. "I'm still concerned about the other night, Sophie. I really want you to get a CT scan and see a neurologist."

"Oh, come on, Andrew, why do I need to do all that? It wasn't a big deal."

"Mom, you were walking down River—"

"Excuse me, but is your name Andrew?"

"You didn't remember why you were there or how you got there, Sophie," Crawford said. "We need to make sure you're okay."

"Oh, I know how I got there," Sophie said under her breath.

"I'm sorry, Sophie; I didn't hear that."

"Never mind. I'm telling you, it's all these damn medicines. If you—"

"We need to make sure it's not something else," Crawford said.

"Like Alzheimer's? Why don't you just say it?"

"Because that's not what I meant. Yes, Alzheimer's disease and other forms of dementia are causes of memory lapse, but—"

"It was more than that, Dr. Crawford," interrupted Roz. "She was acting a little bizarre if I have to say so."

Crawford nodded. "As I was saying, there are many other causes as well. We need to think of everything. And that's what neurologists do."

Crawford looked to Roz. "Okay? Are we all set? Let Barbara know if you need any scrips."

"Let me just make sure before we leave." Roz had made a list and started making little check marks next to each note. "We'll get the clotting studies here now, I'll schedule the CT scan today, and you'll give me a referral to a neurologist."

"How about some Xanax? You all are really getting to me, you know. And don't think I'm not serious."

"See Kuchinsky," Crawford said, as if he hadn't heard her. "Alan Kuchinsky. He's on Wisconsin Avenue. He's very thorough."

Roz jotted his name in her notebook and closed it. "She does need more Lipitor and Vasotec." Then looking at the doctor with a slight nod toward Sophie, "And she's going to cut back on the wine. Right, Mom?"

"One glass, Sophie," Crawford said. "Think of all that sugar. I think that's what's making your glucose go up."

━┤ ├━

"I'm sorry, Mom, but I don't think it's appropriate to call a doctor by their first name. He spent a lot of years in school and in training to get where he is, and it's disrespectful."

"He's younger than me. He's Andrew. And if that's disrespectful, then tell him and all those bimbos in his office to start calling me Mrs. Horwitz. I've spent a lot of years getting to where I am."

Roz sighed and shook her head. "You know, Mom, you're getting to be rather difficult."

"No one asked you to come today, Roz. I could have driven myself."

Roz pulled into the basement-parking garage of the twelve-story medical building on Wisconsin Avenue. The lanes were narrow, and she engineered the Mercedes sedan around and around until someone finally pulled out near the rear entrance into the lobby. She shut off the engine and looked straight ahead for a moment. Finally she spoke.

"You stayed on Long Island for a while after Dad died, and you weren't very happy. We all agreed it would be a good idea for you to move down here. Part of the reason was so that we could help you as you got older. I can't help it if you need help, Mom. What do you want me to do, leave you alone? Let you take a cab to all these appointments?"

"I can drive, Roz. I'd really like my car back, so I can get myself around. And I don't know who you're referring to when you say 'we all agreed' for me to move down here, but I don't think 'we' included me."

"The last time you drove you missed the entrance to Westwood and ran into a ditch. Last week you were out walking on River Road at midnight. How can you responsibly drive a car? How can I responsibly *let* you drive a car?"

"It was dark and raining—you know that. Like you've never missed an entrance."

Roz gathered her purse. "Why don't you come up with me? I really don't want to leave you alone in the car."

"Then you should have taken me home and called the office like everyone else does."

Roz shook her head. "I have things to do, too, you know. It works better this way."

"You mean when you're in their face?"

No response.

Sophie leaned back in the seat and closed her eyes. "I'm telling you, Roz, don't have them fit me in today. I've had enough already."

Roz put the front windows partly down, got out, locked the car doors, put the keys in her purse. "I'll be right back," she said. "Don't get out."

Sophie closed her eyes. Somewhere deep in her skull, in the middle of the right side of her brain, the throbbing was back. Whoosh, whoosh, whoosh. Soft and steady, in beat with her heart. Not quite pain, not quite pressure. It was a deep noise that was somehow alive, breathing and beating in her head. She had first noticed it a few weeks before when they were playing Texas Hold 'Em in the park. It had surprised her enough that she'd missed her bet and lost to Lily of all people. Since then it had happened a few more times, always eventually dissipating on its own or with help from caffeine or alcohol or Xanax. She opened her eyes. It wasn't even noon yet. Caffeine it was.

There was a coffee shop in the lobby of the medical building. She picked up her purse from the front seat floor and moved to unlock the car door. The lock was silent, unmovable. She swore, looked over at the driver's side door, spotted the lock control. Placing her purse in the driver's seat, she leaned way over, reached the lock control, pushed it, and fell back into her seat. With a deep breath, she unlocked the door and got out.

Now what? Leave Roz's Mercedes unlocked? No. She'd lock it and wait for her in the lobby. She locked the car, shut the door, turned for the lobby. Damn! She turned back around. Purse sitting on the front seat, mocking her it seemed. Damn, damn, damn! She eyed the passenger side window for a moment. Worth a try. Roz had left it open enough to give her plenty of air. She put her arm in and reached way down. Straining, she got an index finger on the lock button and pushed it. Next thing she knew she was stumbling backward, her hands covering her ears. The shrill biting alarm sounded over and over, piercing the air and banging off her eardrums like little jabbing knives. She kept moving, backward, out of the way, out of blame. On and on it shrieked. Passersby in the garage stopped and looked her way. A parking attendant stepped out of the parking-toll booth. Sophie kept moving until she was at the rear door of the lobby. The attendant looked around and headed for the car. Sophie opened the door and disappeared into the lobby.

The lobby was busy with people milling around the elevators and going in and out of the pharmacy and coffee shop. Though the car alarm was muted through the cement and steel, she could still hear its rhythmic shrieking. She looked at the elevators, all the while moving toward the front door that opened onto Wisconsin Avenue, one of the main arteries flowing into Washington, DC. At the door she stopped and stared at the elevators. Roz was probably going to step out any second. She could tell her she just needed some air, or to stretch, or coffee, or…It didn't matter. She'd still be listening to it all the way home and the next day and the next and…

She found herself outside, moving and merging into the early-lunch crowd that was easing down the street. She straightened her blouse, tugged on her skirt. Without the familiar weight of her purse on her arm, she felt awkward, almost undressed. She watched the faces going by—surely they could see that she was not properly attired, that no sane woman would be walking down Wisconsin Avenue without a purse. She kept her arm bent, as if it were there, as if just the appearance would deflect any suspicion. No one seemed to notice, though, and she breathed more easily.

She stopped at a traffic light with a group of ten. Now what? Saks was across the street. She could go shopping, but certainly there wasn't a woman in her right mind who would go into Saks without a purse. She walked another block, came to another light. Her breaths were coming harder now, the whooshing in her head faster, stronger. There was a Starbucks across the street, and she crossed in the crosswalk with the others.

Besides not having any money, she had no phone. She desperately wanted to call Val. She looked around—maybe she could use a phone in one of the stores. Most of the shops were high-end boutiques, and she hesitated. Then she spotted a chain clothing store where she had shopped once with her granddaughter and... all the people around her were looking down Wisconsin Avenue. She turned. Long blue beams of light were slicing silently through the air, cleanly parting the pedestrians nearest to them as they moved slowly down the street. For a moment she could not see their source. Then the traffic moved a little, and she saw the police car in the curbside lane across the street. It was moving a few feet at a time, its laser-like beams scattering people in their wake as if the beams were indeed weapons, yet all the while eerily silent.

It was the silence, the emergency without an emergency, that froze her, that instantaneously took her back. Holidays, anniversaries, birthdays—ten years later, they all came and went now, often without much thought of Martin. Or if there was, it was just a few blurred sequences strung together, brief and devoid of much visceral emotion. But not now. Her stomach turned with the same stabbing jolt of fear she'd felt when she'd turned the corner into the YMCA parking lot and had seen the commotion of flashing lights and milling people. The instant roiling in her stomach, the somehow knowing that this was for her and that it was not good, for the lights were silent! Whatever rush for life there had been had passed. Without the sirens the flashing wands were just a show of power, a warning to all that life and limb were always just a tenuous existence.

And she'd been right, though she'd tried to avoid it. She'd parked her car away from the ambulance hoping to go in a side door, hoping to simply pick up Martin and avoid the trouble. But an elderly man whom she'd recognized as a swimming friend of his saw her and said something to one of the police officers who immediately headed her way. She'd started to cry then, silently. She hadn't even seen him that morning. He was having trouble with his eyes and wasn't driving, so one of his friends in the swimming exercise class had picked him up. To save her a trip. And now…

He was practiced at it. "Mrs. Horwitz, I'm so sorry, but…he didn't suffer…massive heart attack." Her world was spinning, tilting. She'd heard the police officer at the same time that she'd seen the Martin-less future, the life she'd thought of from time to time but not really.

She had to go to the emergency room to make things official and to say good-bye. There, in an exam room, Martin lying on the ambulance gurney covered head to toe with a white sheet, a nurse had kindly uncovered his face. It was bluish-gray and frozen in a look of surprise and anger that had taken her back for a moment. "Oh, baby," she'd said, stroking his hair. "Oh, baby."

The police car now came abreast of her, and she could see the officer inside scanning the street. She merged back into the crowd and headed for the Starbucks at a normal pace. Slipping inside, she stayed by the window for a moment and watched the police car cruise slowly out of sight. This was not good. The emergency without an emergency. For a moment she felt a wave of nausea deep in her stomach and a longing just as deep to have back the last ten minutes of her life. Another police car came into view, and she moved away from the window. Serves her right, she said to herself. She could have called the office for an appointment like a normal person.

She went to the bathroom, patted some warm water on her face, adjusted her blouse, took a deep breath, went back out. On one of the counters near the front of the store, she found a *Washington Post*. She folded it, put it under an arm, went up to one of the baristas.

"Miss, do you think you could do me a big favor?"

"Sure, how can I help you?"

"My daughter's picking up a blouse at Saks and will be here in just a minute. My purse is in her car. Do you think I could go ahead and order, and we'll pay you as soon as she gets here?"

"Absolutely," she said cheerfully. "What can I get for you? Do you want to order something for her, too?"

"Umm, sure. She'll be here in a sec. We'll both have grande regular café au laits. Extra hot please."

"Whole milk?"

"Please. Thank you. You're very kind."

"No problem." She shouted out the order to another barista making drinks and looked to a man who was next in line. Sophie moved away and found a table where she could see through the front windows. Blue lights flashed by again. She unfolded the paper and started to read the Style section.

The words, however, would not stay in focus. She put her face in her hands, closed her eyes, tried to think. Whoosh, whoosh, whoosh. Somehow she had to get a hold of Val.

"Regular café au laits, extra hot," yelled out the barista.

She picked up the coffees and sat back down. If she got back to her room, she could pretend she'd been asleep. She could pretend she'd gotten tired and had taken a cab home. She'd had money in her blouse, of course. Even these days, what self-respecting woman went out without cab fare stashed away in her bra? Yes, she had to get home before Roz looked there.

She stood and went over to an older man who was sitting alone, cell phone out on the table. "Excuse me, but my phone just died. Would it be possible…"

He handed her the phone, and she turned away from him and dialed the only phone number she had committed to memory.

"Where the hell are you?" Val said. "You've really done it now. Roz is going nuts."

"I know, I know. I'm sorry. It's a long story. Can you come get me? *Please.*"

"I'm already in my car looking for you. Like the rest of the city. Where are you?"

"In the Starbucks down the street from Saks. If you pull up out front, I'll run out. I need to get back to Westwood before Roz gets there. "

"I'm not far away. I'll be right there."

Sophie gave the phone back and sat down, one eye on the door, the other on the barista. She gulped one coffee as fast as the heat would let her and started on the other. Whoosh, whoosh, whoosh. Val's Lexus stopped out front; the barista turned to help a customer. Sophie was up, out, and crying as soon as she hit the seat.

"What in the name—"

"Don't," she said, putting up a hand. "Just take me home, please. I can't take this anymore."

LILY

Val turned restlessly in her bed and put her arm around a pillow. Jules was toying with her, as he often did deep into the night and the early morning. One moment his eyes and smile beckoned her to him; the next he was looking off, showing only the back of his bald scalp, golden again in the setting sun. She was sitting next to him, leaning back in one of their old beach chairs, sand covering her feet. For a while it was enough, a physical presence she could almost feel. Then, as if she knew there were only so many more of these nights, she became impatient, lusting for more. In the last year some new door in the darkness had opened and taken her closer to him than she'd ever been since he'd died. Some nights she could taste his lips, smell his skin and breath, feel the coarseness of his chest moving over hers.

She reached out and touched his arm. His big head slowly turned, and he leaned close to her. So close that she could smell him now, the dried sweat on his neck, the beer on his breath. Her chest tightened, and the sinewy, graying muscle of her pounding heart picked up its pace, battering at its bony cage. Then he was gone, and she was wide awake, her chest fluttering like the sparrows that banged frantically in the eave beneath her roof. She closed her eyes and tried to bring him back. For a minute she lay perfectly still, feeling him around her, on her, inside of her. But he would not come to her now, could not come to her now. Sun was filling the eastern window, and the incessant rapping in her chest was getting worse. For another minute she lay still and thought about her day. Then all she could feel and hear was the thumping of her heart. It was time to get up. She needed to take her medications, and Lily, whether Lily remembered or not, was waiting for her.

"Good morning, Mrs. Kantor. How are you today? You look nice—I love your blouse."

"I'm well, thank you. And you, Petra?"

"I'm good. Mrs. Preston is in the dining room. Would you like to join her?"

"Yes, please. That would be nice." Val looked at her watch. "We have a few minutes. Her physical-therapy appointment is at ten. We should leave by nine-thirty or so. You know how the parking is over there."

"Do you want to sign out now? Her daughter knows you're taking her, right?"

"Yes, of course. She was quite grateful. She has a meeting today."

Petra put a clipboard in front of Val, and she signed the page-long release absolving the Towers Assisted Living Facility of all responsibility for Mrs. Lily Preston once she set foot out the door with Val. Other than Lily's family, Val was the only person authorized to sign for Lily.

"Let me know when you leave, Mrs. Kantor. I need to write the time down."

"Sure. We'll say good-bye on the way out."

Val adjusted her purse and headed to the dining room. She was fairly tall, five-nine or so, and only a few pounds over the weight she carried in her twenties. She stood tall as well, carrying herself with the air of the healthy, which in this facility immediately marked her as a visitor, a doctor, or one of the staff. So it was that whenever she walked into the Towers dining room, most of the residents would turn her way and stare. Each time it was the same; each time she pondered the same questions as she headed toward Lily. Did they wonder if she was there for them? And if she was, for what reason? Perhaps she was a new doctor or a relative they did not remember. Or worse, she could be their doctor or family member they were supposed to know or expect. Were they cognizant of such things? Was there more behind the blank stares?

Val paused in the middle of the room. About half of the tables were occupied, some residents sitting up on their own, some with wheelchairs pulled up to the edge of their table. As with most nursing homes or assisted-living facilities, there were four to five women for every man. In fact, looking around, Val saw only two men eating breakfast. One seemed to be asleep, his chin on his chest; the other was staring suspiciously at her. Lily was where Val knew she would be—in the corner near the largest bay window. Although Lily preferred to sit alone, the staff did not believe this was healthy for her social skills, and they would almost always put another resident at her table. A bent woman in a robe was sitting in a wheelchair across from her staring into her plate.

Lily was sitting straight up in her chair looking out the window, her hands folded in her lap. She wore a white silk blouse buttoned to her throat with a delicate gold pendant resting on her chest. Beneath the pendant were two small fresh orange juice stains, and Val grimaced to herself. White was not Lily's best color these days, but it was her favorite, and she had a whole closet full of white silk blouses. Lily turned toward her as she approached the table. For a moment she just stared, and Val felt the morning ebb out of her.

"Good morning, Lily," Val said. "You look wonderful." And she did, despite the orange juice. If Val was only a few pounds over her youthful weight, Lily, perhaps, was less. She, too, was tall, about the same height as Val. Her hair, an elegant shade of gray streaked with shards of silver, was full and pulled back with a single gold clip. She had been raised in Georgia in a town and time where ladies did not sit on the beach or beside a pool, and the skin of her face and hands was smooth and nearly spotless.

Val sat next to her and looked into her eyes. Once a rich sapphire blue, they were now a dull shade of gray, the pupils clouded with early cataracts.

Lily took one of Val's hands and put it between hers. "Val, it's so nice to see you, dear."

"And you, too," Val said, putting her other hand over Lily's.

"I love your blouse, darling," Lily said, taking a finger and running it down Val's sleeve. "You know a good blouse. You certainly do."

"Not like you."

"Oh, don't you say that, honey. You're always so sweet."

"Are you ready to go, or would you like some more coffee?"

Lily looked at her.

"Your physical-therapy appointment is at ten. Julie said I could take you. Remember, you asked her yesterday."

"I remember, honey. Of course I do." Leaning over, she whispered to Val, "Let's go before we get old." Lily looked across the table at the bent woman who now looked like she was sleeping and actually shook her head. "For heaven's sake, I swear she's going to fall right into that plate."

Val stood, reached over the table, pushed the plate away from Lily's dining companion. Then, taking Lily's arm, she said, "Sophie's waiting downstairs. Let's say good-bye to Petra and get the heck out of here."

⊨⊰ ⊱⊨

"Well, if it isn't Miss Georgia Peach."

"Sophie, dear. It's so good to see you."

"What'd you do, order Belgium waffles and cappuccino? Geez, Louise, I think I had another birthday out here."

"Have you been waiting for us, honey? I'm sorry."

"Have I been waiting? It's gonna be ninety damn—"

"Oh, stop it, Sophie," Val said, shooting her a dirty look. Then to Lily, "You know how these New Yorkers are. Hurry up until you die, and then you were rushed."

Sophie made a disgusted noise and turned back around in the front-passenger seat. "Well, that's one thing I'll guarantee you. I certainly won't tell you I was—"

"*Sophie*," Val said, giving her another look. "It's a beautiful morning, we have Lily for at least a few hours, and we're going to have some fun."

"What kind of appointment do I have?" Lily asked.

"PT," Val answered. "But you just got sick. Too bad."

"I do feel just *awful*," Lily said, settling into the back seat.

Val was already on the phone. "Hello...Yes, this is Mrs. Kantor. I just wanted to let you know that Mrs. Preston isn't quite up to her physical therapy today. I might run her over to Dr. Banford's... Oh, sure, I expect she'll be there Monday. We'll let you know if she can't make it...You're welcome. Have a nice day."

"You're scary," Sophie said. "How about some coffee? Let's go to Starbucks and hang out for a while."

"Absolutely," Val said. "I want to try one of those new tea things, and I haven't seen today's paper yet. Then I think we should go to the park. It's not too hot yet, and there's that great table that's shaded. What do you think, Lily?"

"I do feel awful," she said. "I'll tell Julie myself."

"I'll take care of Julie," Val said. "Don't worry about that." She looked at her watch, changed lanes, headed for downtown Bethesda. "In fact, we're going to do that right now, so we don't have to worry about little Miss Julie. Crystal will get you in and out."

"Oh God," Sophie said. "Banford's office is a zoo. We'll never get out of there."

"She doesn't need to see Banford. Relax, I promise. Crystal will have her in and out of there in no time." Val looked in the rearview mirror. "So what about the park, Lily? What do you think about sitting in the shade and playing cards?"

"That sounds just fine, Miss Val." Lily had been looking around the car for the past few seconds. "Where's Goldie?"

"She's getting ready for Frank's service," Val said, looking in the rearview mirror again. "Remember, I told you he died this week."

Lily looked out the window. "Yes, of course, dear. I've been thinking about her."

Sophie turned her head. "That's nice, Lily. What have you—"

Val hit her arm, and Sophie turned back around.

"We need to order flowers," Lily said. "For Goldie."

"I already did, Lily," Val said. "I sent them from all of us. You'll see them on Friday—they're beautiful."

"Three hundred bucks," Sophie said. "They better be beautiful."

"Oh, my. Three hundred dollars. I don't know if I—"

"My treat," Val said.

"Part of the plan," Sophie added, turning in her seat again to face Lily and smiling for probably the first time that morning. Then, the smile quickly gone, "Mo's back in the hospital. It's just us today. But that's one of the things we have to do. We gotta figure out how we're gonna get her out of there for the service. At least she's out of the ICU. That'll make it easier."

"Which service are you speaking about, Sophie?" Lily asked.

"*Frank's* service, Lily. Remember—he *died*. He's d-e-a-d dead. It's this Friday. Say it to yourself three times. Frank—Friday, Frank—Friday, Frank—Friday."

⊷⊶

The early morning rush at Starbucks had cleared and the mid-morning crowd—women in exercise clothes, retirees, the unemployed looking through want ads on their laptops—were quickly taking up the few tables and stools. Val bought a *Washington Post* and Sophie, limping and moving slowly, circled the tables trying to shame someone out of one. After all, her face seemed to say that she was an octogenarian and they were not. It worked fairly quickly, as it usually did. A young man who'd been alone at a table for four got up and offered her a chair. When he saw that Val and Lily were with her as well, he politely picked up his newspaper and went to sit at the counter along the wall.

Val ordered a new Asian tea and got Lily her usual black coffee. Sophie had ordered a café au lait with whole milk, extra hot, and stood by the espresso machine watching the barista as if she knew he would do it wrong. When he handed it to her, she felt the cup, gave it back, and asked him to heat it up a little more.

"You keep doing that, and they're not going to let us in here anymore," Val said to her as they walked back to the table.

Sophie had two cardboard wraps around her cup and steam was coming out the top. "I can't help it if he's got wax in his ears," she said. "I told him extra hot to begin with. It's no accident he's working here, you know."

"Maybe he's paying his way through school. You never know."

"I know he's got wax in his ears and a bumblebee on his butt."

Val pushed the Style section across the table. "Here, look at this, and tell us if there are any good shows in town."

Val's cell phone rang. She took it out of her purse and looked at the caller ID. "Uh-oh, it's Julie."

"Maybe you shouldn't answer it," Lily said, fidgeting with her fingers.

"I have to," Val said. "Otherwise she won't let me take you out anymore."

"Hello…Oh, hi, Julie, is everything all right? Yes, of course she's with me. Sitting right beside me as a matter of fact. She wasn't feeling quite up to her PT this morning."

Val put her hand over the phone and whispered to Lily. "She thinks you're faking it. She thinks you don't like going to PT." Then to Julie, "I don't think so, Julie. She felt a little light-headed, so I didn't think it was a good idea to force it. I took her over to Dr. Banford's, of course. Crystal checked her out and said she was fine. Her blood pressure was one-forty over ninety. We gave her some juice, and she felt better…you mean right now…we're headed for the park. Dr. Banford said she ought to get some air. Actually, he really thinks she needs to be outside more. He's not sure she's getting enough Vitamin D."

"Oh, that's a good one, Val," Sophie said, sipping her drink and scanning the newspaper.

Val put a finger up to her lip and smiled. "Yes, I'm sure she's fine. You can relax. We'll just sit there and chat for a while…of course I will. I always put it on her. Forty-five, in fact. She really likes that new Neutrogena one that my dermatologist recommended…Yes, I realize there's a fine line between her getting burned and getting enough Vitamin D." Val shook her head and rolled her eyes. "And don't worry, I won't keep her out too long. Go ahead and go to your meeting. Everything's fine."

Val ended the call and patted Lily's hand. "Julie's going to check on you later. She said to make sure you took it easy today. And to make sure I put sunscreen on you."

"No wind sprints today, Lily," Sophie said, still looking at the newspaper.

Val laughed and started reading again.

"Excuse me for a minute, please," Lily said. "I need to use the powder room."

Val looked up. "Do you know where it is?"

"It's in the back, sugar. Past that machine. Isn't that right?"

"Right. It's on the left as soon as you get past the counter."

Lily stood, and Val looked at Sophie for a moment. They watched her make her way to the back of the store before going back to the newspaper.

Lily, they knew, was always rather meticulous in the bathroom. First, she would check her hair and blouse in the mirror. Then it would take her a while to actually use the toilet. In her younger days, she would squat so that her skin never touched the seat; now that she could no longer squat long enough, she would cover the entire seat with toilet paper, or a prepackaged toilet wrap if it was available. Either option was a pain-staking process. Then when she was done with all that, it would take her a while to wash her hands and adjust her blouse and hair again.

Five minutes at least, they figured.

"Maybe I should go check on her," Val said, five minutes after Lily had left the table.

"She's okay," Sophie said without looking up. "She's just primping."

Val looked to the back of the store, but the hallway was blocked with customers standing near the espresso machine. "There's a door back there, you know. It goes out to the back of the shopping center."

Sophie looked down the hallway. "If you turn that way, it doesn't look at all like out here."

"I know, but she could have forgotten where she was."

"She's not that bad."

"I'm going to go check on her."

"Okay. Yell if you need help."

It wasn't a yell, but it was as close to one as Val was going to emit in Starbucks. Startled, Sophie looked up to see Val rushing toward her. Val grabbed her purse off the chair and headed to the back again, talking as she went. "She's gone. Go out the front door and go left. Stay on the sidewalk and look for her there and in the parking lot."

She pushed through the back door, turned, paused. Starbucks's trash bins were to the left of the store, in the back, so she figured Lily would have almost surely turned right. She turned right, scanned the rear parking lot. No sign of Lily. She headed toward the walkway that cut from the rear parking lot through the shopping center and out to the front. When she reached the walkway, she looked around again and then ran toward the front sidewalk, her purse flapping against her side. Twenty yards short of the sidewalk, she had to stop, her chest suddenly tight and her breaths short and rapid. She paused for a few seconds and then started walking as fast as she could. She reached the sidewalk, stopped, saw Sophie down to the right, turned left. She passed a few small boutiques and the pharmacy. She was still rushing, still breathing hard, her chest pounding. People on the sidewalk turned her way, but she did not seem to need help, so they simply watched her brush past. A group of women in front of her separated to let her through, and there was Lily about forty yards ahead looking in a store window, her hands folded in front of her as she did whenever she was waiting. She turned and looked around but didn't seem to notice Val who was now approaching her at a normal pace.

When Val got close enough, the first thing she saw was the fear in Lily's eyes. Though her face was perfectly calm, her hands were still folded in front of her and her eyes were wide open and full with the panic of a lost child. Seeing Val they started to tear.

"You silly-willy," Val said, putting an arm around her and hugging her. "You got turned around and went out the back door."

"I'm so sorry, Val. I must have gotten confused."

"It's easy," Val said. "The doors look exactly the same." She took Lily by the hand and started slowly moving up the sidewalk. "Come on, let's find Sophie."

Lily took a tissue and wiped her eyes. "I'm sorry, Val. I really don't know what happened."

Val hugged her again. "It happens, Lily. Forget it. We're going—"

Sophie limped into view, stopped, shook her head. "Thank God," she said. "I wasn't going to be the one to call Julie. Where'd you go, Lily, window shopping?"

"As a matter of fact, she did," Val said, steering them toward her car. "There's a great outfit in the window of that Pink store. Come on, let's go to the park before it gets too hot."

⚊⟡⟡⚊

Sophie called the game—Seven Card Draw, one-eyed Jacks wild. She had just dealt and was picking up her cards when Lily looked at her and said, "I've been thinking about what you said, Sophie."

Sophie was losing and had not said anything for several minutes. She looked at Val and then back to Lily.

"What'd I say, Lily? I don't remember."

"About dying. About what we'd like to do before we died."

"I don't think she said it was about dying," Val said. "I think it's more about living." She raised an eyebrow at Sophie when Lily wasn't looking. "While you still can, what would you like to do while you're living?"

"Oh bullshit," Sophie said. "Maybe I didn't come right out and say dying, but it's all about kicking the bucket, and you know it. This isn't family time, you know—you don't have to talk like you're in therapy."

Lily drew a card and looked at Val. "I'm sorry, sugar, but I'd have to agree with Sophie. It's just another piece of passing on. I've lived plenty long enough."

Val looked at her cards and was quiet.

"So?" Sophie said, looking at Lily.

"I believe it's Val's turn, darling," Lily said.

42

"Right. But what about what I said?"

Lily looked at her for a few seconds. "Oh, you mean about the dying?"

"Yeah, the bucket, Lily. The bucket."

Lily looked down at her hands, folded them, unfolded them. "You might think this is silly, but I want to go back to Sea Island. I'd like to sit on the porch by the ocean and…" It was Lily's turn, and she drew a card. "No help," she said.

Sophie looked at her, but Lily was quiet. "Why don't you finish, Lily?"

"I did. I don't have a darn thing, honey."

Val's cell phone rang again. She spoke for a minute, then closed it, and smiled at Lily. "That was Crystal. Julie either didn't believe what I told her or she wanted to hear it all again for herself. Including the bit about you needing to be out more."

Lily's eyes clouded the way they did when she got angry, which was a rare event. "If that woman spent half the time on her own children that she does worrying about me, she'd be a lot better off."

"She is a little hyper," Sophie said. "She might even be worse than Roz, and that's pretty damn bad. You need to talk to Walker about her."

Lily seemed to smile. "Walker is his father's son," she said softly.

"What do you mean, Lily?" Sophie asked. "Of course he's his father's son."

Lily was quiet for a moment. Finally she said, "He doesn't like to talk about trouble."

"We'll take care of Julie," Val said, putting a hand on Lily's. "Don't you worry about her. So, what were you saying about Sea Island? That's what I want to hear about. Something about sitting out on a porch by the ocean and…"

GOLDIE

I t was Val's general experience that not only were hospitals usually rather inefficient providers of health care but they fared
even worse in the personal service department. She had reached
this conclusion after managing her own husband's illnesses and
death and shepherding innumerable friends through emergency
rooms, cardiac suites, and oncology wards. She had also served as
a nurse with the air force and worked for years in various health-
care consulting capacities. Other than emergency care when one's
functional life was actually salvageable or the inevitable intermit-
tent admissions such as Mo's, staying out of hospitals was always at
the top of her priority list.

This particular morning was no different. According to the
plump ward secretary who was multitasking a super-sized soda and
a stack of patient hospital charts, neither Dr. O'Connor nor any of
his staff had notified St. Joseph's, or specifically anyone on Ward 5
East, that Maureen Flanagan was to be discharged that morning.

Val did her best to look perturbed yet patient. For in all fair-
ness to Dr. Francis O'Connor, it was not his decision, and he was,

in fact, unaware of the impending discharge. Even if he had been, at age seventy-eight and about five years past the point when he probably should have stopped practicing internal medicine, Dr. O'Connor often didn't remember the little things from day to day. Val had spoken with him the night before when he had come to see Mo in her room, and, although they had talked about Mo going home soon, he hadn't quite said that she was to be discharged in the morning.

Val and Sophie had decided that. Frank's funeral service was in five hours, and Mo was going to be there.

"I'm sorry, I don't know what happened, but I was in her room last night when Dr. O'Connor told the nurse to discharge Mrs. Flanagan in the morning. I don't remember her name, but I would probably recognize her."

"They're all gone now."

"I realize that," Val said, keeping her voice even but adding a slight edge. "So, we can do this one of two ways. You can call his office and speak with Cheryl, his head nurse, or I'll call her and have her call you."

"It's very busy right now. Why don't you have the office call us and give us the order again? There's a phone down in the quiet room."

Val looked at the unattended phones spaced around the work area and back to the secretary and took a measured breath. "Thank you," she said calmly. "I would be happy to call the office. I'm sorry, would you tell me your name again, please?"

"Sasha. But they can call any of us."

"Okay, Sasha. Thanks."

Val moved down the counter, turned her back to Sasha, and tapped on her cell phone where Dr. O'Connor's office number and key extensions were stored.

"Ma'am, you can't use a cell phone on this ward. It can interfere with some of our equipment."

Val moved away from the desk as if she hadn't heard Sasha.

"Hi, Cheryl? This is Mrs. Kantor. I'm over at St. Joseph's with Mrs. Flanagan. I'm sorry to bother you, but Dr. O'Connor told one of the nurses last night to let her go this morning, and you know how that goes." She turned around and headed back toward Sasha. "I'm taking her home for Mary Catherine, and I'm here at the hospital. I guess the secretary forgot to put the order in. She's all set with her medications and everything. He told her what to do last night, so they just need a verbal order. I know he's busy. Would you mind just telling the ward secretary that it's okay...that's great. Thanks so much. She'll be in to see him Monday or Tuesday. Hold on—I've got her right here."

"Sasha, I've got Cheryl from Dr. O'Connor's office on the phone." Val reached over the desk and extended her cell phone.

With a sigh, Sasha took the phone and the order and went back to work. "I'll tell her nurse in just a minute," she said, handing the phone back to Val without looking at her.

"Thank you," Val said, turning toward Mo's room and scanning the hall for a wheelchair. Twenty yards past the elevator, tucked into an alcove, she found one with the hospital's name imprinted on the back of the blue leather.

She parked it outside of Mo's room, knocked once on Mo's door, and then walked in without slowing. "Up and at 'em," she said cheerfully.

"Are you sure it's okay? I don't want to get in trouble. Mary Catherine will kill me. And you."

"Dr. O'Connor discharged you, dear. Come on, let's get dressed. Sophie's outside, and we still need to get Lily."

"What about Mary Catherine? You know she's going to have a seizure if—"

"Don't worry, I took care of that. You'll see her later today."

Val took one last look around to ensure that there were no IV lines or tubes going in or coming out of any of Mo's body parts. "You're taking fluids, right?"

"Depends what they are," Mo said with a grunt and a grimace as she sat up. For a moment she sat still, her eyes closed.

"Are you okay?"

"Yeah, it's my back. It hurts like holy hell."

Val looked at her. "You don't have to go, you know."

"Oh, I'm going all right. We're going out to lunch, too." Mo stood up, holding onto Val. She moved to the mirror and straightened her wig. "Nothing that a little makeup won't fix."

"I brought you a dress."

"You went to the house? Are you—"

"I brought you a *new* dress. Not too slinky, not too nunnish. Just right for a class act like you at a funeral." Val took out a one-piece navy-blue dress from the garment bag she had brought and held it up to Mo. "Perfect. You're a star."

Mo didn't like to cry, at least openly. Sometime around fourth grade, a now faceless, nameless nun had wiped that emotion out of her. Instead, her eyes would get moist and glisten, and her lower lip would tremble.

"Shhh," Val said, putting a finger on Mo's quivering lip. "Don't say a word. Let's get out of here."

Val was unbuttoning Mo's nightgown when the phone beside the hospital bed rang. She stopped for a moment and looked at it. "Don't answer it," she said to Mo, slipping off the nightgown. "Here, I brought you some stockings, too. Let's get these on and get you dressed, and we can work on your makeup later."

"But—"

"Shhh. You're not going to see anyone you know on the way out to the car."

"That's what you think. Half my Sodality group's in here."

The ringing stopped and then started again. Val never slowed. She helped Mo put her arms in the dress and then moved behind her to zip it. The phone kept ringing, again and again. Finally it stopped.

Val quickly went through the drawers in the nightstand and checked the closet. "I have your night bag and the clothes you came in. Anything else?"

Mo straightened her wig again and smoothed out her dress. "I don't think so."

A nurse came in. "Your daughter's on the phone, Mrs. Flanagan," she said. "She said she's been calling you. Is everything okay? Why are you dressed like that? You're not going home, are you?"

Mo looked to Val.

"She's fine," Val said, "but she really has to pee. Will you please tell Mary Catherine she'll call her back as soon as she can?" Val took Mo by the arm and led her into the bathroom. "Dr. O'Connor discharged her last night," she added over her shoulder. "I'm pretty sure the night nurse did her paperwork with her. She doesn't need anything. She's all set with her meds and her follow-up appointments."

"That's funny, they didn't say anything about that when we changed shifts."

"I think there was some confusion last night," Val said through the open bathroom door. "It was pretty busy." Then sticking her head out, "Please tell Mary Catherine that she'll call her back as soon as she can. But don't tell her she's going home or that I'm here—we're going to surprise her. It's her birthday."

Val closed the door and shook her head. "Lord, we'll never get out of here." Putting Mo on the toilet, she said, "Just stay here until I get back. I have to go get the wheelchair. And don't tell me you don't want one. It's just until you get to the door. Hospital rules."

Mo smiled for the first time that morning. "Oh, that's funny. *Hospital rules.*"

"Zip it," Val said, smiling. "I'll be right back."

A few minutes later, the hall clear of nurses, Val wheeled Mo out and toward the elevators as fast as she could push the wheelchair.

Sophie was waiting at the side entrance with Val's Lexus. "Geez, I thought I was going to run out of gas. You stop to eat breakfast, or what? Hi, Mo. Wow—you look great. Val told me she got you a dress, but she didn't say it was a…a *dress*. I'm going to have to change. Maybe at least put on some heels."

"You're fine, Sophie," Val said. "You look great. Besides, we'll probably be the only ones there."

"You never know. Some rich old bastard might be on the prowl. I'll do anything to get out of Westwood. And I mean *anything*."

"If he's rich and old and alone, then he probably is a bastard," Val said.

"Yeah, who cares? They're all bastards."

Val helped Mo into the back seat and took over the wheel.

"You do," Val said. "This is a big day."

"Oh, okay. You know I'm just kidding anyway. I don't put out for just anyone, you know."

"*Sophie*," Mo said, giggling. "Don't talk like that."

"You're right, Val; it is a big day," Sophie said, her face suddenly serious. She looked at Val; Val looked back and shook her head in affirmation.

"What are you two talking about?" Mo asked.

"We're now officially all widows," Val said.

Sophie looked out the window.

Val's cell phone rang.

"Mary Catherine," the three of them said together.

Val checked the caller ID—Mary Catherine Dunn.

"Hello," she said…"Oh, hi, Mary Catherine…We're on our way to pick up Lily, and then we're going to Frank Tannenbaum's funeral. Actually, I think I told you in the e-mail that the funeral was at noon, but it might be at one…I sent you an e-mail last night about Mo being discharged and all that. It was too late to call, and I know you check your e-mail all the time…Around ten-thirty or so...Oh, my, I understand why you're worried. Gosh, almighty, I'm sorry. I thought you knew about everything...To your regular address. Hold on a sec; let me double-check it."

Val took the phone from her ear, set it in her lap, and winked at Sophie. Ten seconds later she picked it up. "McDunn at AOL dot com...*you changed?* Oh my gosh. I think I do remember that. I'm so sorry. I guess I forgot to change it. I'll send it to you again when I get home, but let me fill you in. Dr. O'Connor..."

Val hung up and looked at Mo in the rearview mirror. "You need to be home by three. Four at the latest."

Mo made a noise and looked out the window.

Sophie looked at Val for a moment and then slowly shook her head and smiled. "You sent it to the wrong e-mail address on purpose, didn't you?" she said. "And then you're going to forward it to her, so she'll see you really did send it." Sophie nodded again and grinned even wider. "They don't have diddly-squat on us, do they?"

"Nope. Not even diddly-squat."

Every table at Jean Michel's was full. The white linen tablecloths were crisp and spotless; the crystal glasses sparkled in the full late-morning sun as if they were alive, flashing like cups of diamonds. The small intimate restaurant was often noisy when it was busy, but now it was particularly so, a cacophony of voices and clinking glass and silverware filling the room.

Val looked around the table and smiled. "Cheers," she said, holding up her water glass. "Here's to Goldie."

"To Goldie," they said in unison.

"Is she okay?" Mo asked. "Have you spoken with her?"

"She's fine. She said to say hello, and she's looking forward to seeing everyone. She's trying to find a way out of sitting shiva for the whole time."

"She's been sitting shiva for the last year if you ask me," Sophie said. "Maybe longer. Frank was half-dead when I first met him. She ought to get some credit for all that time." She thought about it for a moment. "One day's enough. She gets six days off for the last six years, and then we get her the hell out of there."

"I'm working on it," Val said. "The problem is she's not sick. She's in the best shape of all of us."

"Here's to you, Miss Val," Lily said, raising her water glass. "Thank you for a lovely morning."

"Here, here," Mo said, raising her glass to Lily's. Then she said, "What do you think, Sophie? Are you going to have a glass of wine? What the heck. I think I'm going to have a bloody mary."

Sophie had turned to the wine list. "You know," she said slowly, "I think I am going to have a glass of wine. I'm going to have a glass of this Kenwood Sauvignon Blanc." She looked at her watch. "In fact, I'm going to have it at eleven forty-five in the morning in honor of Dr. Andrew Crawford."

Val looked at Lily and rolled her eyes.

"What about you, Lily?" Mo asked. "Do you want a glass of chardonnay? Maybe a mint julep?"

Reaching out with her leg under the table, Val stepped on Mo's foot. "Lily," Val suggested, "why don't we hold off for now? We'll be the responsible ones in the group."

"Iced tea would be fine for me," Lily replied.

"That's right," Sophie said. "Ladies don't drink before noon. Guess that counts us out, Mo." She reached across the table for a high five from Mo and then picked up her menu. "Val's treating," she said, "so don't be shy."

"Why, thank you, Val," Lily said. "That's very kind of you."

"You don't always have to treat us, Val," Mo said. "We can pay sometimes."

"I want to," Val said. "My pleasure."

"Part of the plan," Sophie said.

"Shhh," Val said. "Now, what do you think looks good? I had the crab salad the other day—it was very nice. The asparagus plate is also…"

The waiter came and took their drink order.

"I wish I knew what this plan is that Sophie keeps talking about," Mo said. "How about you, Lily? Do you know anything about this plan?"

Lily took a sip of water and fingered her gold pendant. "Well, I do know that there is a plan. I've been thinking about it some more. I believe I would like to go back to Sea Island."

Mo looked at her for a moment. "Oh," she finally said. "Well, uh…" She turned to Sophie and then Val. "I guess I'm the only one who doesn't know the plan."

"There's no plan," Val said. "Sophie and I just joke sometimes about how we spend our money. You know, just to drive our kids nuts. Lily's talking about something different. We were talking the other day about what we'd like to do if we only had one more chance to go somewhere or do something."

"You mean like before we die?" Mo asked.

Sophie raised her eyebrows and smiled, but stayed silent.

"No, not necessarily," Val said. "I think of it more as living. Where would you want to go and *live* for a day or a week or whatever? What would make you the happiest?"

"And I said Sea Island," Lily said. "That's where Walker and I went on our honeymoon."

"Good God, Lily," Sophie said. "Can't you think of something better than that? You didn't even like him. I'll bet you hadn't slept with him in twenty years."

"Stop it, Sophie," Val said sharply. "If that's what makes her happy, then leave her alone."

"Yes, that would make me happy," Lily said, her cheeks full of a pink flush.

"You're right. I'm sorry, Lily. I'd just like to forget my first wedding. My second one was pretty good, though. We went to Atlantic City and lost all our money."

The waiter returned, served their drinks, took their lunch orders. Val told him that they had a funeral to attend and were on somewhat of a time schedule. Mo told him to check back with them soon.

"We'll let you think about it for a bit, Mo," Val said. "Let's get ready for this funeral. I don't think there will be many people there, so we might be front and center. We'll have to be on our toes."

Mo took the oversized hunk of celery sticking out of her glass and swirled her bloody mary. Taking a sip, she said, "Oh, that's good. Nice and spicy. How's your wine, Sophie?"

"Yummy. Okay, Val, let's get this over with."

"Who's the funeral for?" Val asked.

"Frank," Sophie said. "Got it, Lily? Frank, Frank, Frank."

"Frank-Friday," Lily said. Then with a sudden smile, she said, "Frank-Friday, Frank-Friday."

"*Friday?*" Mo said. "His name's not Friday, is it?"

"It's Tannenbaum, Mo. Frank *Tannenbaum*. Friday's a joke."

"Married to?"

"Goldie. Come on," Sophie said. "We're not that bad."

"Age?"

"Older than God."

"Eighty-seven," Val said. "He was eighty-seven."

"Brothers and sisters?"

"All dead," Sophie said.

"Correct. How about Goldie's family?"

"One sister and Goldie hates her," Sophie said. "She won't be there."

"Why not?" Mo asked. "She's her sister."

"'Cause they're stubborn *Jews*, Mo. They *hate* each other."

"I know, but…"

"We're not talking about Catholic guilt here, Mo. There's about as much chance of her being there as the Pope."

"Please don't talk about the Pope like that. You know it upsets me. And you shouldn't say that other word either. It's not nice."

"What do you mean? 'Jew'? Jesus, I'm a Jew. Sort of. I can call a Jew a Jew."

"Children?" interrupted Val.

"Two boys," Sophie answered. "They're okay, but she isn't real hot on either of their wives."

"Names?"

"Christ, I don't remember their wives' names. Do you?" Sophie asked. "Geez, Louise, I'm eighty-three."

"Her sons are David and Howard. I don't remember the wives' names either. Rachel is one, maybe. Goldie has that friend she visits in Florida, too. Rhonda, I think it is. She might be there. They're pretty close."

The waiter returned with their food.

"Okay, that's enough," Sophie announced, sipping her wine. "We can fake the rest."

Mo finished her bloody mary and asked the waiter for another. "Poor, Goldie," she said. "I hope she's okay. How did he pass?"

"He just stopped breathing," Val answered. "It was time." She hesitated a moment and then added, "Maybe you should slow down a little on the bloodies, Mo. We have a long afternoon."

"I thought you said he had a stroke," Sophie said abruptly, pulling apart her crab cake and inspecting the filling.

"Stroke, respiratory arrest. Maybe both. Who knows? What's the difference? Dead is dead."

Sophie turned her crab cake over and inspected it again. "There's a difference," she said, looking at her plate. "A big difference."

"Were you there, Val?" Mo asked. "It must have been so awful."

"Yeah, she was there," Sophie answered. "Imagine that. She was right there with him when he croaked."

Val cocked her head and looked at Sophie. "What is that supposed to mean, sweetness?"

Sophie held her gaze for a moment and then went back to her crab cake. "Oh, nothing. Dead is dead as you say."

"Yes, it is, sweetness. Especially for Frank." Val lifted her iced tea. "To Goldie. Bon appetit!"

Sophie looked around the parking lot. "Are you sure this is the right place?"

"I told you there wouldn't be many people here," Val said. "And I told *you* not to have that second bloody," she said to Mo over her shoulder.

"I really have to go," Mo said. "I don't know what it is—maybe all those IVs."

Val rolled her eyes and got out of the car. "Sophie, do me a favor and go find the bathroom. I'll help Mo out. Lily, you stay with me."

"They filled me up like a water balloon in there," Mo said, biting her lip. "I think I'm going to go right here, Val. I can't help it." She unlocked the door but wasn't strong enough to push it open.

Val reached her, lifted her legs, swung them out of the car. Taking hold of her under her armpits, she half-pulled, half-lifted her out.

Mo grabbed hold of the door and steadied herself. Her face stiff with pain, she stayed still, her eyes closed. When she opened them they were glistening in the morning sun.

"You gotta hold on," Val told Mo. "You can do it."

They hurried up the sidewalk, Val holding tightly onto Mo's left upper arm.

Sophie came out. "Oh my God. Goldie looks great. I saw her in the waiting room. You know that hot little black dress she wore to the Kennedy Center—"

"Where's the bathroom, Sophie?" Val interrupted.

"Okay, okay. Down the hall on the left. How does she stay so skinny? Everything I eat goes right to my hips. I knew I should have—"

"Please get the door, Sophie."

"Oh, Val," Mo moaned, trying her best to speed up.

"What's the matter with her?" Sophie asked, watching Val almost drag Mo through the door and rush down the hall.

"Mo needs to use the powder room," Lily said.

"You think?"

"I hope she's all right," Lily said, standing erect in the hallway, her hands crossed over the small purse she held in front of her. Then softly, she said, "I'm afraid she's not."

Sophie watched them turn into the bathroom and looked at Lily. "Have you ever been to a Jewish funeral?"

"I don't believe so," Lily replied after a moment.

"Just follow me. It's not much different really, except you won't understand anything once the rabbi gets going." She glanced one more time down the hallway. "They might be in there a while. Let's go see Goldie."

Goldie was standing in a room adjacent to the synagogue proper. Other than two middle-aged couples sitting across from her, she was alone. Seeing Sophie and Lily, she opened her arms and moved to hug them.

Stepping back, she said, "You both look so nice. And I so appreciate you coming." Lowering her voice to a whisper, she added, "I think the rabbi and my sons were worried there wasn't going to be anyone here. Pretty much all of Frank's friends are dead, you know. A lot of mine, too." She looked behind them. "I thought Val was coming. I know Mo's in the hospital."

"Oh, they're here all right," Sophie said. "We got Mo out this morning. She's in the ladies room primping. You know how she is," she added, with a little smile at Lily.

"Mo's not like that at all, Sophie," Goldie said. "You know that. Right, Lily? She's not like that at all."

"No…no, I don't believe she is, Goldie."

The rabbi had come in and was waiting for Goldie.

"Let's get this show on the road," Goldie said to the two of them. "Let me introduce you to my sons, and then you go inside and have a seat. Give Val and Mo a hug for me. And listen, don't you even *think* about going to the cemetery afterward. It's way too hot. Go to the park and play cards. I'll see you this week." She lowered her voice again and winked at them. "Soon as I get out of sitting shiva."

Sophie and Lily chatted with Goldie's sons and their wives for a minute, and then everyone was asked to move inside. With no sign of Val and Mo, Sophie and Lily took seats as far back as they could without seeming rude. That was the third row, the closest seat Sophie had ever had in any place of religious observation other than her two weddings.

Besides Goldie and her sons who were up front on seats beside the rabbi, there were maybe ten other people in the synagogue. Goldie's daughters-in-law were front and center; a few single male and female octogenarians were scattered in the front rows; two elderly couples sat together in the second row.

Everyone seemed to turn when the rear door opened. The rabbi, already into his opening comments on Frank Tannenbaum's life and virtues, stopped, started, and then stopped again as Val and Mo made their way down the aisle.

Sophie had wisely saved them the two end seats. Holding onto Mo's arm, Val deposited her in the seat next to Sophie, mouthed, "I'm sorry," to Goldie, and sat down.

Mo started to make the sign of the cross, but an elbow from Val stopped her with her hand still on her forehead. "I can still pray for Frank, can't I," Mo whispered under her breath. "Is that not allowed in here?"

"Shhh," Val replied. The rabbi was making a poignant point about Frank and everyone was shaking their heads in agreement. "Just shake your head and pray to yourself. One day without the sign of the cross won't kill you."

Sophie was looking at Mo's legs. "I thought you had stockings on, Mo," she whispered.

"They got a tear," Mo replied, not looking at her.

"Shut up, Sophie," Val said, as quietly as she could, which was still not enough. Both of Goldie's daughters-in-law looked over at the four of them and then back to the rabbi.

The rabbi motioned for the mourners to stand. Val looked at Mo.

"Jesus, Mary, and Joseph. I…I don't know if I can stand right now."

Val put a hand on her shoulder. "It's fine. Stay right where you are."

The rabbi began to chant in Hebrew and the mourners bowed their heads. After a while there seemed to be a natural break in his singing and Val started to sit, but then he started up again with new vigor, his strong, lyrical voice resonating through the room.

Val folded her hands and looked to Goldie, who was standing with her eyes closed. She closed her own, taking herself back one, two, three, almost four years now. Four years that seemed like a month; four years that flashed before her in a kaleidoscopic blur where the end merged right back into the beginning. She had met Goldie playing bridge through a series of women friends who were now either dead or near dead. They'd been matched up as partners, which for a whole year had been a deadly combination. Then Frank's dementia and other illnesses had worsened, and Goldie wasn't around as much with taking care of him and her trips to Florida when she was struggling and "needed a break."

Lily had joined the group next. Val was tempted to open her eyes and look at her, but, at least for the moment, it wasn't the Lily she wanted to see, although outwardly she looked exactly the same. In her quiet Southern way, Lily had been as sharp as Goldie, luring her opponents with her languid voice and manners as if it were not possible that guile and trickery could also exist in the same body.

Mo came shortly after Lily, within the first year or so after her husband died. She loved to play cards and enjoyed her wine and slipped into the group effortlessly. She was healthy then, still in her old house and going to daily 7:00 a.m. mass. Two other bridge groups and her sodality group took up most of every day. That and the wine helped her manage all the memories of Michael Flanagan, particularly the morning he lay dead in his bed alone.

Sophie was the last to join the group when she moved down from New York after her husband had died. She'd met Val in Starbucks as they'd both silently eyed each other over a vacant table. They'd both caved in and sat together, and they'd been almost inseparable since then.

A noise from beside her opened her eyes. Val blinked, accommodated to the light, and looked around. It came again—a nasal grunt from beside and below.

A few heads turned. Val and Sophie looked at each other for a moment and then down to Mo. Her head was bent, her chin almost on her chest. Before Val could reach down, Mo's chest expanded and deflated, and a guttural snore ripped through the room.

Except for Goldie and the rabbi, every head turned their way. Val quickly reached down, lifted Mo's chin off her chest, held it up until Mo opened her eyes. It took Mo a few seconds to focus, and then looking startled, she asked, "What's the matter?"

"You fell asleep, honey. It's okay. I don't think it'll last much longer."

Mo didn't respond. She looked to Goldie, looked out to the aisle, bit her lip, which was starting to tremble.

Val put a hand on her shoulder and kept it there. Leaning down, she asked, "Are you okay?"

Mo shut her eyes and clamped down on her lip as if she were in pain. The rabbi droned on. Val turned Mo's chin toward her with a finger—a tear had leaked out of her eye and was sitting on her cheekbone. Squeezing Mo's shoulder, Val whispered, "Talk to me, Mo."

Mo opened her eyes, now full of tears. "I gotta go again, Val. I can't help it."

Val straightened and looked around. The daughters-in-law and the assistant rabbi were looking at them again.

Val looked at Mo, looked at Goldie, reached for her purse. Taking out several twenties, she pressed them into Sophie's hand. "We'll be outside. If I'm not there, take Lily home in a cab and *make sure* she gets to her room. Then you take a cab home. *Straight* home, hear me?"

The rabbi had stopped and was waiting for Val to finish. "I'm sorry," Val said, loud enough for Goldie and him to hear. "She's not feeling well." Val took Mo by the arm and lifted her up.

Goldie had moved off the podium and was waiting in the aisle. She hugged Mo, told her not to worry, and hugged Val.

"Oh, Val," Mo said, moving up the aisle. "Oh my God, it's coming out. Oh my God!"

VAL

"You're killing me, Val," Scott Yureman said, rubbing his eyes. "Not only do I have a financial responsibility to you, but you know my ass'll be grass if you run out of money. Bill will flip out. I could get sued for Christ's sake. It's been done before, you know."

"Scott, the last time I checked it was my money. It's my name on the trust—not Bill's, or Debbie's, or Roger's."

"I know, Val, but geez, can't you just slow it down a little. I cut you a ten thousand dollar check last month, and we're headed for the same this month. Christ, I can't make the market go up. I can't raise your dividends."

"There's plenty of money, Scott. I'm not going to live forever. And I'm not going to live like a pauper, so my adult children can go on vacation."

"You're only eighty, Val—you could live another twenty years for heaven's sake." Yureman picked up the spreadsheet on his desk and shook his head. "Right now I see us headed for trouble in ten years. And that's if nothing really bad happens. Geez," he said, rubbing his eyes again, "it could be five."

Val looked out the window and looked back. "I'll be eighty-two next month, Scott. I really don't think you have to worry about ten years from now. I just don't know if I can stand all this fun anymore."

"Oh, come on, Val. For heaven's sake, you weigh less than my wife, and you look great."

"Do you have my check, Scott? I have to go to the doctor again, and then I have to go pick up a friend. She really has run out of money. Would you like to know why?"

"Sure, Val, why? Because her investment advisor didn't perform his fiduciary responsibility?"

"No, that's not why."

"Because she spent more than she had?"

"No, Scott. That's not why either. She ran out of money because her husband was a gork and lived to be eighty-seven, which was about seven years too long. He was on thirteen prescriptions. I can name them for you if you want. It cost her almost a thousand dollars a day at the end. She's headed for the street." Val paused and looked out the window for a long moment. "Thank God he died," she said, turning back. "Goldie couldn't take it anymore. I couldn't take it anymore."

"No kids around?"

"Children are not responsible for their parents' financial problems, Scott. Yes, she has two sons. That's where she'll probably have to move. Do you really think she wants to move in with her oldest son and a daughter-in-law she can't stand?"

"Well, you're not responsible for her either, so don't get any wild ideas."

"May I please have my check, Scott?"

Yureman pushed a check across the desk and sighed. "You're killing me, Val."

"You'll live, Scott. I promise you. And you'll be okay."

Yureman grunted and said, "By the way, so you know, Bill wanted to come today. He's concerned about how much money you're spending; I told him he had to ask you. I guess he didn't."

"Well, Scott, if you really want to stay out of trouble, then I would strongly suggest you don't talk to Bill about my finances without my permission."

"I didn't, Val. I can't believe you would—"

Val stood up. "See you next month, Scott." At the door she stopped and turned around. "And just so you're not surprised, I may need more money next month. A lot more. I might be going on a trip."

"A trip?" he said as Val turned once again to leave, his voice trailing after her. "You're killing me, Val. Do you hear me? You went away last month. Six grand, remember? Six grand in one week. A trip. Shoot me, will you?"

Val had three new voice mails plus the old one from Bill, her oldest son, to which she still hadn't listened. He called most days that he knew she was seeing Scott Yureman, always fishing for an invite. The executor of her estate since Jules had died, he, too, was the champion of fiduciary responsibility—his own and Kristen's, the money-grubbing wench of a wife he had insisted upon marrying. Bill's calls, she knew, were as much from her prodding as his own interests. And supposedly he was also looking out for his siblings— the quiet Debbie and the troubled Roger, who actually could use whatever money was left when she died. She felt for Roger and had often thought of changing her will, but the fighting and ill feelings would be too much to stomach. At least for now.

She deleted the message from Bill and listened to the new ones: Roz, asking her to call about Sophie; Mary Catherine, asking her to call about Mo; Julie, asking her to call about Lily. She looked at her watch—later. The morning was sitting on her like a ten-pound weight, and she hadn't even seen Dr. Bernstein yet. And Goldie, she was sure, was counting the minutes.

Walking through the entrance to Dr. Harold Bernstein's office, she felt the same leaden weight sitting on her, pulling her down. She was tempted to turn around and head right back down the elevator and out, out, out, but the ramifications—Bernstein's nurse calling Bill or Debbie yet another return visit—forced her to the check-in desk and then to a worn, faux mahogany chair. She guessed there were three octogenarians in chairs around her and a hunched over man who had to be approaching his century mark.

She closed her eyes and tried to think about how she was going to help Goldie, but her mind kept returning to the three calls she had yet to field. She was still dealing with the repercussions of Mo arriving home in a urine-soaked dress, Lily being unceremoniously let out at her building in a cab, and Sophie arriving home at three in the afternoon with alcohol on her breath. But she could not think above the noise emanating from her chest. Thump, thump, thump—faster and faster. Thump, thump, skip, thump, skip, thump. Concentrate. Goldie was waiting; three unanswered calls were waiting. Thump, thump, skip, thump.

"Mrs. Kantor."

She opened her eyes, took a deep breath, went into the small nurses' room. Down a pound—frown from Sandy. Heart rate 108—bigger frown. Blood pressure 150/96—shake of Sandy's head.

"Do you feel okay?" Sandy asked, stepping back to look at her.

"Peachy."

"Fibber."

"Swear on a Bible."

"We'll see—he's ready for you."

Dr. Bernstein had his stethoscope on her chest for a full minute, moving it around as if he were playing checkers. Finally, he took it off her chest, pulled the earpieces out of his ears, and looked at her.

"How do you feel?"

"Peachy."

"Any chest pain? Are you short of breath at all?"

"I'm peachy, Harold. Do you want me to spell it?"

"Your rate's up, and you're missing a lot of beats. More than before. You need an EKG. We need to adjust your meds, too."

"I had an EKG two weeks ago, Harold."

"Yeah, well, you weren't tachycardic and as arrhythmic as this two weeks ago. I'm not making it up, Val."

"Okay, Harold, I'll get an EKG. I need some scrips. Do you want to write them or do you want me to?"

"Funny, Val. Very funny. You need to double your atenolol and your Vasotec. You need to eat more, too. You're down another pound."

"I need Zoloft, Xanax, and Sonata. You need to double those, too."

"Val, it hasn't even been a month yet. I told you—I can't keep writing all those prescriptions for you. Can't you get your shrink to write them?"

"You are my shrink, Harold. I thought you took care of the whole body."

"Seriously, what happened to your shrink?"

"Harold, what in God's name does an eighty-two-year-old woman need a shrink for? I'm orgasmic, okay. Even now if I want to be. Technology's great these days."

She watched Bernstein's face turn pink and went on.

"I was married. Twice. I was actually happily married. Okay, I'll give you that one. I was happily married once."

"I think you're depressed. You've been depressed ever since Jules died."

"Jesus, Harold. Everyone's depressed. If you're not depressed, then you're dead."

"See—you do need a shrink."

"Zoloft, Xanax, and Sonata, please."

"You're going to get me in trouble, you know."

"Pick your poison, Harold. You can write my scrips or I can jump off the balcony, which is right into the Beltway by the way. You can explain it to Bill."

Bernstein sighed, took a prescription pad out of his white coat, and started to write.

"I'm serious, too, Harold. Double them."

⭠⭢

Goldie was waiting outside of her building, her cell phone to her ear. Seeing Val, she turned sideways, spoke for a few more seconds, and then ended the call.

"Oh my God, where have you been?" she said, almost hopping into the front seat. "Get me out of here before David gets here."

"Shiva's going well, I see."

"Shitsva is what it is. I've been sitting shitsva for ten years. I'm done. I even told them so. Let them sit there and stare at each other. I mean, *really*? All his friends are dead, and I see enough of that family."

"It does seem a little redundant."

"As if they really care that much anyway. The truth is they're both pissed off because they have to pay for the funeral and get my car out of the shop."

"Where are we going?"

"Out of here. I told them I had an urgent doctor's appointment. That actually does get you out of sitting shiva, you know. You feel like shopping?"

"Always. Where?"

"The mall. I need to get a few things."

Goldie's phone rang. She checked the caller ID and ended the call.

"You can take that if you want. I don't mind."

"It's okay. It's just David."

66

Her phone chimed softly and a text came up. She glanced at it, closed the screen, turned it over in her lap.

"You sure?" Val said. "I really don't mind."

"Dead sure."

"Whatever you say," Val said, watching her out of her peripheral vision as she pulled up to a stoplight. Goldie had turned the phone back over and on and was scrolling to what Val thought was her Settings screen. Then the light changed, and the phone was back over.

Montgomery Mall was quiet in the late morning. Val and Goldie had shopped together a lot and had a routine. Park outside of Macy's, wander through the top level, sample the perfumes, and get a free makeup do-over from the Lancôme bimbette or, if she had already been used up, from whatever new chicklet was hawking Estée Lauder or Clinique. Stroll out into the mall proper, check out the diamonds, and browse through the Apple store and check out the new iPhone or iPad. Besides Val, Goldie was the only other one among the five of them who was interested in new technology. Goldie, in fact, had taught Val a lot of what she knew about iPad navigation and many of the nuances of their new iPhones.

Not today, though. Goldie seemed to know where she was going, and it wasn't meandering through Macy's. She led Val past the cosmetic kiosks, out into the mall, down the escalator. Stopping in front of Victoria's Secret, she put a hand on Val's arm.

"Please help me, dear. I want sexy but not too skanky."

Val just looked at her. "What?"

"Oh, come on, Val. You're no prude. I'm a free girl now. Help me out, will you? The hell with those old cotton things."

"Okay, free girl," Val said, smiling for the first time that day. "Sexy, maybe even a little sleazy, but not skanky."

"You got it."

Goldie took her arm and led her into the store. She stopped at the first rack of lace underwear and started flipping through the smalls. There were several saleswomen milling around, but it took a minute before one came over.

"Do you have something in mind?" she asked. "Maybe I can help."

"Yes, please. Sexy but no skank. Black."

"Do you know what size you're looking for?"

Goldie just looked at her for a moment. "Honey, I'm eighty-one years old. If I don't know what size I wear by now, I might as well buy Depends now shouldn't I?"

"She's looking for herself, dear," Val said as the girl flushed.

"I'm sorry. I didn't mean—"

"It's okay," said Goldie. "I'm old, but I'm not that old. I like black. Sort of see-through I think. Particularly the bra. Small undies and 36B."

The girl smiled and seemed to brighten at the thought. "Why don't you look over here," she said, turning toward a different part of the store. "These are some of our best sellers. Sexy but not too—"

"Slutty," said Goldie. "I don't want slutty or skanky. I want sexy. There's a difference, you know."

"Goldie," Val said. "She sells sex—she knows."

"I don't know, Val. The girls these days, all they see is skank. Do you ever watch HBO? Let me tell you, I do. *Sex in the City* started it. And it's been all downhill from there." They were weaving their way around racks of multicolored undergarments, Goldie talking over her shoulder. "I don't think they know how to act anymore. They just give it out to anyone." She looked at the saleswoman. "I don't mean you, dear. I'm sure you're a very nice girl." Looking back to Val, she said, "I don't think they really know what *sexy* is."

"I liked *Sex in the City*," Val said. "Is that such a big deal?"

The girl had stopped them at a rack of matching bras and panties and looked from Val to Goldie, her eyebrows crinkled somewhere between surprise and laughter.

"I did, too," Goldie said. "Loved it, actually. But it's been all down-hill from there. Holy moly—I watched that Hemingway thing on HBO last night. Talk about hot. Except she was a real skank."

Val shook her head and rolled her eyes at the young woman.

The girl pulled out three sets of black lace underwear for Goldie to try on. Goldie looked at Val and then at the girl. "Honey, would you please come in with me and tell me what you think. I really don't think my friend wants to see me naked. She's already been to the doctor today."

"I'll pass," Val said. "Do you want me to hold your purse?"

"Please, dear. I won't take long."

Val watched them go into the dressing room and watched the door close. Goldie's purse slipped down her arm, and she moved to adjust it and then paused with the flash of light from the top of the purse. She opened it slightly—Goldie's phone was lit and facing her. A phone message flashed silently on the screen. Val frowned. She had never seen Goldie turn off the sound on her phone let alone ignore calls, even from David. She moved behind the rack of lingerie and took out the phone—missed call from Saul. Saul? Hmm.

She stared at the phone for a moment, then tapped on the phone icon, and tapped on recent calls—five that morning from Saul, the most recent of which was twenty seconds ago. The next twenty minutes before. That was the call in the car, she quickly calculated. The call before that was most likely when Goldie was on the phone waiting to be picked up. Tap on the arrow next to Saul—all from the same number with a 239 area code. She followed more calls down the screen: David, Howard, Saul, Saul, Val, David, Saul at midnight.

Val stepped around the lingerie and looked at the closed dressing room door. Tap—text messages:

Saul, at 11:00 p.m. the night before: pls call when you can, miss u.
Goldie: David's leaving now. Call you in a few. Miss u, too.
Val: pick u up at 11.

No other text messages. Another frown. She had texted Goldie several times the day before, so Goldie was deleting.

Check the door again—closed. Tap, tap—voice mail. Twenty minutes ago from Saul—not listened to yet. Better not mess with that. Midnight—last night, from Saul. She paused, feeling her stomach roil. Tap—"Hi, honey. I'm sorry I missed you. I've been thinking about you all night. I can't wait to see you and hold you. I love you."

Her head was literally spinning. She reached out and took hold of the aluminum bar in the rack of see-through bras. Her head steadied. Tap, tap—Settings—sound off, text alert off.

Tap—e-mails. She heard the door open and then Goldie's voice. No time. Tap one last time back to the main screen, drop phone in purse, step out from behind the rack.

Goldie was smiling. "She's good," she said. "I'm going to take all three. You find anything?"

Val shook her head no and frowned slightly. "Are you...are you sure you want all of them?"

"Yep. Are you okay? You look a little pale."

"I'm okay. I think I'm just getting hungry."

Goldie reached for her purse and headed to the counter. "We'll go eat as soon I pay for this," she said.

"I've got it, Goldie. My treat today." Val took out a credit card and put it on the counter.

Goldie took the card and handed it back to her. "Val, please." She dug deep into her purse and took out a stack of hundred dollar bills with a rubber band around it. She peeled off three and handed them to the cashier.

Val looked at the inch-thick stack of bills, looked at Goldie, raised her eyebrows.

"Honey, you don't really think I'm *that* naïve, do you?" Goldie said.

"Umm, I guess not."

"Honey. *Really?*"

TWO

The idea is to die young as late as possible.

Ashley Montagu

SOPHIE

"Yes, Roz, I do understand she needs the CT scan—that's why I called you. And of course because you asked me to, so if there's anything else you want to talk about that's fine, too. I really don't think there's anything to worry about with that problem at Westwood, though."

"I certainly hope not. And at some point, I would still like to know what happened at the funeral. Velma said Mom came home in a cab, and she smelled like a winery. I can't deal with that now. I'm ready to fall apart as it is."

"Mo wasn't feeling well, Roz. I almost had to take her to the hospital. I thought the cab was better than dragging Sophie around with me."

"I do understand that part. I'm just worried about her drinking. I'm starting to think she has a real problem."

Val, sitting in the front seat of her Lexus, pointed to the phone and mouthed silently to Goldie, "Yeah, you." Then on her Bluetooth, she said, "Roz, I'm not sure a glass of wine at lunch qualifies as a drinking problem."

"Well, if it was only one, it might be okay. I don't think she knows when to stop, though. We can talk about it later. I have to deal with this today. If she gets away with this, then she'll do it for everything. I swear to God—and don't you dare tell her this—but we're really close to moving her in with us. We can't take this constant worrying. Every time the phone rings, it's like what's next? It's worse than having a teenager."

"Oh no," Goldie said before she could help herself.

Val leaned across the front seat and put a hand over Goldie's mouth.

"What was that, Val? I couldn't hear you."

"Sorry, it's the radio. I'm in my car. I'll turn it off. I need to keep you on the speaker, though." She put a finger to her lips and mouthed, "Shhh" to Goldie.

"So will you please call her and see if you can get her to come to her senses? You're the only one she'll listen to these days."

"She has a mind of her own, Roz—you know that." Val winked at Goldie and put her finger to her lips again.

"Her appointment is in an hour. You don't know what I went through to get that."

"I'm happy to call her, Roz, but it might be better if I took her over there today. I think I can talk her into that. It would also give us a little alone time in the car, and I'll try to talk some sense into her as you say."

"Then she just gets her way, Val. She's like a little kid. That's just rewarding her. She has a neurology appointment Wednesday— she'll do the same thing with that."

"I know it's frustrating, Roz, but she'll get the CT scan done, and isn't that what we all want?"

Silence.

"Let's get this done today, Roz. We'll deal with the neurology appointment next."

"I don't know, Val. You have better things to do, and I'd like to be there."

74

"Okay. Give me a minute to call her, and then you call. And I'm sure you don't have anything to worry about with that other thing. They'll turn up."

Val hung up and dialed Sophie. "Morning, sweetness."

"Don't start with me, Val. I'm not—"

"Stop, Sophie. Roz is going to call you in a minute. Just tell her you're not going, and then she'll let me take you."

"I don't care if it's you or the Queen of England. I'm not going. How many times—"

"Sophie!"

Click.

Val stared at her silent phone for a moment then. "Five minutes," she said to Goldie. "Maybe three."

"You don't really think she had anything to do with that, do you?" Goldie said.

Val shrugged. "I hope not."

Goldie's phone lit up—text message. She looked at it, closed the message, turned her phone over in her lap.

"David?" Val asked.

"Who else?" Goldie said quietly, looking out the window.

Val's phone rang. "Hi, Roz."

"Okay, she'll go if you take her. Let me know as soon as you're done. I may meet you back at Westwood. I think I'll clean up there a little bit, and then you can tell me about it while we're all three together."

"No problem—I'll call you."

"And please write down everything."

"Of course I will, Roz."

She dialed Sophie. "Ten minutes, sweetness."

"Oh, don't 'sweetness' me. I swear to God I'm not doing it."

"I don't think that would be such a great idea, dear. We'll talk in the car."

"What, do you have wax in your ears, too? I'm not—"

"Ten minutes, sweetness. And Sophie…"

"What now for Christ's sake? Don't tell me I have to go see Andrew, too."

"No. I'm just giving you a heads-up that Roz might be coming over to clean up while you're out. So, if you have anything you might, uh, not want her to see, you might want to put it away."

Silence.

"We'll be there in ten. Bye."

⇒‖‖⇐

"Well, if it isn't Miss Victoria herself," Sophie said, climbing into the back seat. "You get lucky yet?"

Val shot Sophie a dirty look along with a slight shake of her head.

"I told Sophie about our little shopping trip," Val said to Goldie. "I hope you don't mind. I'm trying to get her out of those Hanes she wears."

"Oh, I'll get out of my Hanes all right. They'll come off for the first guy who can walk and talk at the same time. And if he can still get it up, that's even better. I'll get out of them all right. You bet your sweet ass I will."

"Okay, Sophie, that's enough. We get the picture."

"Yeah, and it's not pretty. That's the problem."

"There are pills for that, you know," Goldie said. "Just because you're eighty doesn't mean you're dead."

"Oh, and how would you know, Victoria? Have you been doing one of Frank's friends all this time?"

"Stop it, Sophie! I'm serious. I know you're in a bad mood, but don't take it out on us. Particularly Goldie. For heaven's sake, I just saved you from an afternoon with Roz."

"That's right, Sophie—don't take it out on me. I'm still sitting shiva."

"Oh, that's funny. Do you get many visitors at Victoria's Secret?"

"Sophie!"

"Besides, don't you watch TV at all?" Goldie asked. "I love those ED commercials. I can't believe they actually say 'erection' on TV."

"Yeah, where were all those guys when I needed them? Four hours? Can you imagine? Damn, I was lucky if I got four minutes."

"Okay, enough," Val said. "For heaven's sake, all she did was buy some new underwear."

Sophie snorted. "Yeah, right. See-through underwear. Just let me know if he has a friend, will you. Tell him I'll make it worth his while."

"Stop it, Sophie. Geez, I think you need some Xanax. You are all wound up."

"I'll tell you one thing—I'm not getting in that damn machine without any; that's for sure. Not that I'm getting in it anyway."

Val handed her purse over the seat. "Side pocket," she said. "Just a half."

Sophie uncapped the bottle, shook a few pills out into her hand, selected a whole one, swallowed it dry. Holding onto two other pills, she recapped the bottle and held it up to the light, so she could read the label.

"You okay, Val?"

Val looked at Sophie curiously. "Yes, I'm fine. Why?"

"Well, let's see. The date on this prescription is yesterday, and the prescription is for sixty tablets, and if I had to guess, I would say there are only about thirty in here."

Sophie slipped the other two pills into a side pocket of her own purse.

"Oh, that. Yeah, I put some aside. You never know when Harold is going to crap out on me."

Val turned into the driveway of the parking garage.

"Don't go in there, Val. I told you—I'm not doing it. Let's go have lunch. I need a glass of wine."

Val stopped the car and turned in her seat. "Sophie, listen to me. If you don't get that CT scan done today, you will never get out of Westwood again. And who knows what else will happen."

Whoosh, whoosh. Deep in Sophie's head, stronger and stronger. Whoosh, *whoosh*! Sophie closed her eyes, feeling the throbbing and the pulsing of the big artery banging against her brain.

Opening them, she said, "No."

"'No'? You're kidding me, right?"

"No. I said no, and I mean no. N-O. No."

"Sophie," Goldie said. "I heard Roz myself. She'll make you move in with her."

Sophie just stared at her. "What did you say, Goldie?"

Goldie looked to Val and back to Sophie. "I'm sorry—I shouldn't have said anything."

Sophie looked to Val. Val nodded.

Sophie's door was open before Val had stopped nodding. "Yeah, well, that'll be a cold day in hell," she said and was out and moving down the driveway, her purse swinging from her arm.

"Goddamn it," Val said and started to open her door. Then she said, "Goldie, quick, go stop her. I'll be right there."

Val drove up to the attendant, gave him a twenty, and asked him to park the car. She caught up with Goldie holding onto Sophie's arm halfway down the block. Sophie was crying, her mascara bleeding into the wrinkles below her eyes. The blush on her right cheek was wet and had a tissue swath through it.

Val put her arm around her. "What is it, Sophie? What's the matter?"

"I don't *want* a CT scan, Val. I don't care what it shows. I don't want to know what it shows. Don't you get that? Doesn't *she* get that?"

"Yes, I do get that. I really do. I'm just—"

"No, you don't! None of you do. I get a CT scan and then what? Then I go to another doctor and then another doctor. For what?

So I can live another three years. Don't you get it—I don't want to live another three years! I—"

"Sophie, please listen to me." Val squeezed her tighter. "I really do understand all that. I'm just trying to be practical now. If you don't get the CT scan done, they are seriously considering moving you out of there, and you're not going to be able to stop them. They have that power of attorney now."

Sophie tried to pull away, but Val held her tighter. "Just listen to me please. Get the CT scan done. Who cares what it shows? I'll talk to Roz. We'll go on our trip and get the hell out of here for a while. We can drink all the wine we want. Chase some men. Who knows—whatever. But just get it done today, because it'll be worse if you don't."

Sophie stared at her for a long moment. "Out of here, Val? You promise me? Out of here?"

"Swear on a Bible. And we'll go to the park when you're done here today. Maybe even have a glass of wine. I'll put her off for a while."

"You have wine?" Sophie said, wiping her eyes.

"Is the Pope Catholic?"

"Okay." Sophie reached for Val's purse and then the side pocket. "I need some more."

The radiology technician told Val she had to leave the CT room before they started. Sophie was on her back, her eyes closed in a 0.5 mg × 2 Xanax calm. She put up a hand—Val took it, leaned over, kissed her cheek.

"We'll be waiting for you," Val whispered. "Hang in there."

"I'm worried about her," Goldie said when Val sat down next to her in the waiting room. "What can we do?"

Val shrugged. "Get her away for a little while. She needs a break from Roz."

"Where?"

Val shrugged again. "Wherever we want. You, too. Before you move in with David."

"What makes you think I'm moving in with David?"

"I thought that's what you said the other day. That's what he said, too."

"We'll see," she said, glancing at her phone.

"Okay. Well, we are getting the heck out of here one way or another. Are you going with us?"

"Of course I am. Are you kidding? If I have one more dinner with Rachel, I'm going to throw up."

Val patted her leg. "Good. Just checking. Let me have that, please."

"What?"

"Her purse."

Goldie gave her a curious look and handed over Sophie's purse. It was a big purse, worn brown leather and heavy.

Val opened it and started rifling through the contents. After a minute she unsnapped a side pocket and took out three envelopes of Sophie's stationery. None of them were sealed, and all three were bulging at the bottom. She opened one, took out a small yellow tablet, shook her head. She opened the next one and took out a pink triangular tablet and then an orange oblong tablet from the last one. She moved to put the envelopes back, saw the two yellow tablets in the bottom of the pocket, took them out. For a moment she just looked at them. Then she dropped them back in, put the envelopes back, closed the purse, looked off to the radiology rooms.

"What are those?"

"The two she stole from me are Xanax. The envelopes are Valium, Xanax, and Trazodone."

Silence.

"So, she did take them. Oh my gosh. Why?"

"She's scared, I guess," Val said after a moment. "Once you start on that stuff, it's hard to stop. It makes you even more anxious if you don't have any."

Goldie's phone, face down on her lap, vibrated. She looked at it, paused, finally turned it over. Val could see the caller—Saul.

"I'm sorry, Val, but David won't leave me alone." Goldie stood and put her purse over her shoulder. "Let me talk to him, and I'll be right back."

Val watched her walk toward the door, her phone to her ear. She watched the door open, close. She watched Goldie move into the hall, smile, turn her back to the waiting room. Then she turned back toward the radiology rooms and closed her eyes, feeling her chest tighten. And tighten and tighten.

"Rombauer," Sophie said, turning the bottle of rich honey-colored chardonnay over in her hands. "Vintage is 2016. I don't think we've had this before."

"I read about it in *The Wine Spectator*. It got ninety-two points."

"How much?"

"Fifty bucks."

"That's not too bad."

Val took the bottle from Sophie, poured three glasses, put the bottle back into the soft cooler. "Cheers," she said.

Sophie tapped her plastic cup against Val's and Goldie's and took a long sip.

"That wasn't very convincing," Val said. "Come on, it's over. Cheers."

"Cheers," Goldie said. "It'll be fine, Sophie. Try not to worry about it."

Whoosh, whoosh, whoosh.

Sophie took another sip of wine and rolled it around in her mouth. "Buttery. Maybe a hint of vanilla and oak. I like it."

"Good. I bought a case."

"You going to talk to Roz before she calls the police?"

"Yeah, I guess. I was just putting it off as long as I could."

Val's phone rang. She looked at the caller, put the phone on speaker, set it on the picnic table, put a finger up to her lips.

"Hi, Roz."

"Val, where are you? The radiology office said she was done an hour ago. I've been waiting in her room."

"We're just taking our time, Roz. I'm sorry. I was about to call you. She got a little claustrophobic in there. Getting one of those done is just awful, you know. Have you ever had one?"

"No, but she's had one before. She was fine."

"Not of her head. It's a little different."

"I suppose. So where are you?"

"I stopped to get her some water, and then she really felt like she needed some air, so we just stopped by the park for a few minutes. She's feeling a little better now. Would you like to speak with her?"

Sophie shook her head no.

"Actually, Goldie just took her to the ladies' room. Do you want me to tell her something?"

"I'd like her to come for dinner. Can you bring her to my house?"

Sophie shook her head vehemently.

"Sure, I'll check with her. I'm sure she'd love to if she's feeling up to it."

Val raised her hands in helplessness to Sophie; Sophie was still shaking her head no.

"Okay. I'm going to go home. The radiologist hasn't read the CT scan yet. Did the technician say anything to you or her?"

"No. I asked him, but he said he couldn't say anything until the doctor read it."

"Liar," Sophie mouthed to her. The technician had indeed said he thought there was something abnormal, but he couldn't say anything else until the radiologist officially read the film.

"Darn," Roz said. "Okay, don't keep her out long, please. She needs to rest."

"You are cordially invited to Roz's for dinner," Val said, ending the call.

"I can't believe you said that. I'm sick. You should have just told her I was sick."

"I'll call her back in a little bit."

Sophie drained her plastic cup of wine. "Sick, Val. Sick, sick, sick."

"I hear you, girlfriend. I hear you."

⇥⊢⊣⇤

Val dropped Goldie off, and then turned and headed for the Westwood Retirement home. Sophie's head was back against the headrest, and her eyes closed.

"You okay?"

"No. Does it matter?"

"Yes."

Sophie opened her eyes and looked out the window. "Lasagna," she said. "As if I'm not fat enough."

"Dinner tonight?"

"It's Tuesday isn't it."

"Ah. Would you rather go to Roz's? She knows you're faking it."

"Very funny. I'm not faking it. I am sick. Sick of the whole god-damn thing is what I'm sick of."

Val handed her a pack of gum. "Make sure you use that mouth-wash before you go in, too."

"Yes, Mom."

Val was quiet for a moment. "That's pretty strange what hap-pened over the weekend," she finally said as she pulled into the parking lot.

"Where? What?"

"At Westwood. Roz told me there were some medicines missing off the medication cart. It sounded like a big deal."

Sophie shrugged and closed her eyes again. "Yeah, I heard them talking about that. They probably can't count. You don't have to be a rocket scientist to be one of those aides, you know."

"I suppose."

"Why was she telling you about that? She doesn't think I had anything to do with it, does she? Christ, if I could get my hands on all those pills, I'd take them all at once. Bye-bye," she said, waving her hand at Val. "Nice and easy."

Val looked at her. "Well, don't," she replied. "We're going away soon."

MO

"Val, I really don't know how to say this because you are such a dear friend of hers, but don't you think that letting her drink in the afternoon is a little irresponsible?"

Val rolled her eyes at Goldie and raised the volume on her car speaker. "Retrospectively, Mary Catherine, it probably was. But she'd had a tough few days in the hospital, and she was with her friends and wasn't driving."

"Well, I realize that but still. It was embarrassing for her. And for us, too, frankly."

Val closed her eyes for a few seconds, took a breath, opened them.

"We were mourning one of her best friend's husband, Mary Catherine. It was a little hard to say no. And you know, she is a big girl."

Silence.

"I know that. But I'm responsible for her. And so are you when you take her out of the hospital. Which by the way I still don't really understand. I talked with Dr. O'Connor, and he was surprised she was out. He didn't remember discharging her."

"Mary Catherine, Dr. O'Connor doesn't remember where his office is most days let alone where Mo is. I was there the night before when he told the nurse to send her home in the morning."

"Well, she needs to see him today. And the orthopedist. And she wants to go to Mass. I'm going to have to hire help. I can't keep canceling my appointments."

"I'm more than happy to take her today. You know that."

Silence, again.

"Just let me know," Val said. "I have the whole day free. And I'm sorry it took me a while to get back to you. I've been busy with my family." She looked at Goldie, rolled her eyes again, and prepared to end the call.

"I understand. Let me look at my schedule, and I'll call you."

Val put up two fingers to Goldie as she hung up. "Maybe less," she said, looking at her watch. "And ten to one she wants to take her to Mass and then pass her off. All is forgiven then, you know. The great catholic hypocrisy." Val shook her head and made a noise.

"Must be nice," Goldie said. "Maybe I should convert."

"Why's that, Goldie? Have you been a bad girl?"

Goldie looked out the window.

Val's phone rang.

"Hi, Val. It's me again. Yes, I really would appreciate it if you could take her to her appointments. I'd like to take her to Mass, though. Do you want us to meet you at Dr. O'Connor's office?"

Val shook her head at Goldie in disgust. "Why don't I just meet you at the church? I haven't been to Mass in a while. A little quiet time would probably do me well."

"Oh. I didn't know you were Catholic."

"I'm not," she said, raising her eyebrows to Goldie. "I'm sorry, but is that a problem? I've been to Catholic Mass before. I thought it was okay."

"Oh no, of course it's okay. I, uh, I just didn't understand."

"She likes the ten o'clock Mass now, right? I'll just wait for you in the back."

"Okay. She'll want to sit up front, and she'll stay for the whole Mass. She'll also want to talk to Father Kelly, but I'll try and talk her out of that."

"No problem. Whatever she wants. I'll see you there."

"Oh, and Val?"

"Yes."

"Would you please go in with her to her appointments? She tends to forget things these days. And if you don't mind, would you write down what the doctors say?"

"Sure, Mary Catherine. I can do that."

"I'm not going to any Catholic Mass," Goldie said when Val ended the call. "I haven't been *that* bad. You can drop me off at Starbucks."

"We all just went to the synagogue. What's the big deal?"

"You *had* to go to the synagogue. I don't *have* to go to Mass. I have some phone calls I have to make anyway. That would be a good time to do it."

Val looked at her. "David?"

"Yeah, it never ends."

Val started the car. "Oh, it does," she said. "Just not soon enough."

Father Liam Kelly was speaking to the congregation, his practiced homily voice rhythmic, melodious, somnolent. Val's eyelids drooped, closed. For a few minutes, the church warm and stuffy, she slept. Then some word, some tone, some feeling came alive, igniting a disjointed barrage of images. Faces forming, melting, forming, melting. Henry in her Methodist church, her holding Bill as he was baptized. Jules in church with Debbie being baptized. Then Roger, the thrill and expectations worn down. Mo, four years ago, sitting in the same front pew, dressed in black, the same melodious chants permeating the same warm church. Michael Flanagan, Mo's husband, labor union attorney, church usher, Past President of the St. Patrick's Irish-American Society, resting on his back in a glistening mahogany casket. He'd died in his sleep alone, Mo having moved down the hall years before, which she'd tearfully admitted one day. It was part of why she went to Mass every day before she became ill and now every day that she could get there. She hadn't even known he was dead in his bed until his secretary had called wondering where he was.

The same wooden pew, hard and unforgiving against her back.

A hand was on her arm. She opened her eyes. The rest of the congregation was standing, preparing to pray. The hand on her forearm was the elderly woman's sitting next to her. Val mouthed a thank you, stood, unconsciously mouthed the words of the Our Father with the others. A few more minutes and it was time for communion. She let the people in her pew out into the aisle and sat back down. Ten minutes and one hymn later, Father Kelly ended the Mass and the parishioners started to file out.

Mo was in the front pew, her head bowed. She raised it, made the sign of the cross, reached for her purse. Holding onto Mary Catherine with her left hand and a cane in her right hand, she navigated the aisle gingerly, as if she might slip and fall with any step. She was wearing her wig and her new navy-blue dress with a simple strand of pearls moving gently on her chest.

Mary Catherine was talking to her the entire way or perhaps lecturing it seemed to Val. She was frowning, looking at her watch, shaking her head.

Mo's face lit up when she saw Val waiting at the end of the aisle. "Well, look what the cat drug in," she said brightly. "You're so nice to come get me."

"Yes, she is, Mom, so why don't we just wait until Sunday to see Father Kelly."

Val cocked her head and looked at Mo. "We have time, Mo. Do you want to talk to him?"

"She can wait until Sunday to tell him all her sins. You know she has so many. I don't want her to be late for Dr. O'Connor."

Val looked at her watch. "We have time." Then smiling at Mo and winking, she said, "I mean how long can it take to confess all of your sins, Mo?"

"Oh, Val, it could take a while," Mo said, trying to look serious. "I have not been a good girl."

Val looked to Mary Catherine. "We're fine—really. I'll call you when we're done."

Mary Catherine sighed and shook her head. "Whatever. Just remember to write down what they say, please."

"Of course," Val said, taking hold of Mo's arm. "Ready, dear?"

"Yes, I am."

"Where to besides heaven?"

"Up here to the left. He's doing this just for me, you know."

"He gave a good homily. Very touching."

"Oh, he gives the best. He remembers the way it used to be."

They reached the confessional, and Mo disappeared behind a red, velvet curtain. Although Reconciliation and the Sacrament of Penance were offered face to face, Mo could no more go face to face with a priest in a confessional than she could take a host in her bare hands.

Val took a seat outside and checked her phone. Missed call from Julie. Voice mail from Julie. Missed call from Sophie—no message.

A few minutes later the curtain parted, and Mo came out holding her rosary. Val took her arm, sat her down in the entrance to the church, got the car, helped her out to the front seat.

"Do you feel better?" Val asked as they turned out of the church lot.

"Oh, yes," Mo said. "I always do."

"So, if you don't mind me asking, just what kind of sins do you commit, Mo? You don't have to tell me if you don't want to. I'm just curious. I want to know what I'm missing out on."

"Oh, the usual ones. Nothing too exciting. You know I raised my voice to Mary Catherine or I thought something bad about her or Tim."

"Those are sins? I thought that was normal."

"Well, if you don't have real sins, you have to make up something. Otherwise what's the point in going?"

"Hmm."

Mo was talking to herself under her breath and studying the strand of beads draped over her hands.

"Who are you talking to?"

Mo looked at her curiously. "God."

"'God'?"

"Yes, I'm praying. It's my penance."

"Oh, right. Penance."

"Yes, for my sins. Two Our Fathers and a Hail Mary. I got off easy today."

"Hmm." Val was quiet for a few seconds. "And how exactly does Father Kelly decide your penance? Is there a rule book for sins or something?"

Mo was quiet, her eyes closed. "No, God tells him," she finally said, still speaking softly to herself. "That's why he's a priest."

"Oh. I see." Val turned into the Starbucks lot and parked in a handicapped space. "We need to pick up Goldie," she said. "She's talking to her boyfriend."

Mo didn't seem to hear her. Her eyes were still closed, and she was making the sign of the cross.

⊨⊱ ⊰⊨

Dr. Francis O'Connor, his glasses sliding down his nose, moved slowly from the exam table to a chair. He sat down with some difficulty, took off his glasses, looked at Mo.

"Well, Maureen. We have some problems to deal with. Your endoscopy showed some bleeding in your stomach and a polyp that needs a biopsy. And the CT scan of your spine showed more compression fractures. We already suspected that, but now we know. The good news is that I don't know what that nurse was talking about last week. You're not incontinent, and you don't have an infection. Your urine culture was normal. Are you losing urine at all?"

Mo's cheeks turned pink. "No, I don't think so."

Val wrote: Endoscopy basically normal. CT scan the same. Bladder fine.

"And your daughter thinks you drink too much," he said with a little smile. "I'm sure that's not true, so we'll give you a pass on that one."

"A little wine here and there. That's all."

Val wrote: Wine is not a problem at all. Just limit the bloody marys to one a day.

Dr. O'Connor rubbed his eyes. "You're seeing Chris Sheldon today?"

"At two," Val said.

"I'll let him deal with your back. Let me give you the name of a gastroenterologist. You should have Mary Catherine call this week. The polyp needs to come out soon."

Val wrote: Think about seeing a gastroenterologist. No rush.

"Santini's going to see you this week for your breast, right?"

Mo looked to Val.

"Thursday," Val said, with a little shrug to Mo when Dr. O'Connor was looking at her chart.

"Do you need any prescriptions?"

Val nodded to Mo and gave her an encouraging smile.

"Well, Doctor, I am having trouble sleeping, and...I, uh, I get rather anxious sometimes during the day worrying about things."

Dr. O'Connor looked at her. "That would be normal, Maureen. You have a lot going on."

"Some of my friends take something to go to sleep. Or when they get worried. Not Val, but some of my sick friends. Xantap or something like that."

"I think you mean Xanax." He took out a prescription pad. "A little here and there won't hurt you. Just don't start taking it every day." He wrote out two prescriptions. "Just take a half to start with and see how it goes. And I wrote you for something to sleep if you need it."

"Thank you, Doctor. I probably won't take them at all, but I think it will make me feel better if I have them."

Val wrote: Medications stable. No new prescriptions.

"One last thing, Maureen."

She looked at him expectantly.

"Try and get out and get some air. A little sun would be good for you, too. Not too much, but a little won't hurt you. Your Vitamin D is low."

Mo nodded.

Val wrote: Dr. O'Connor thinks Mo should get away for a little while, preferably some place sunny. Her Vitamin D level is seriously low, and supplements aren't enough. She needs some sun for her bones, and he thinks it would help her all the way around.

"Wow, Mo, that was impressive," Val said as they walked out. "Now you really do need to go to confession."

"Reconciliation, you silly-willy. I'll go on Sunday."

"Whatever. Are you okay?"

"I guess. My back hurts. I really don't want to go see this other doctor. Let's go have lunch."

Val looked at her watch. "I think we have time for lunch. Then we have to go to the doctor or you'll be grounded, and I'll be mincemeat."

"Oh, okay. Do you have any mouthwash?"

"Always. Just one glass of wine, though. And no bloodies. I need you squeaky clean this week. You heard Dr. O'Connor—you need to get away. You need some sun."

⊶ ⊷

"Jesus, Mary, and Joseph," Mo said in as close to a yell as was possible for her. "Oh, please stop, please stop."

"Hold on just another minute," Dr. Chris Sheldon said. In his right hand, he had a ten milliliter syringe full of steroid and lidocaine, the syringe capped with an eighteen-gauge, three-inch needle that was somewhere in the four inches of fat between Mo's skin and her fractured lumbar vertebrae. With his left hand, he was pushing hard on her back to keep her still. He moved the needle again, and she jerked in pain, her eyes shut tight, her lower lip trembling.

"Oh, please stop. Oh, Jesus, please stop."

"I'm almost there, and then it will feel better pretty quickly." He repositioned the needle and pushed it in another inch.

"Jesus, Mary, and Joseph," Mo cried, shutting her eyes even tighter.

Dr. Sheldon finally was comfortable with the needle placement and slowly injected the solution around her inflamed fractures. When he was done, he quickly pulled out the needle and put pressure on the puncture site.

"You should feel better by tomorrow, Mrs. Flanagan," he said. "I'm sorry. I know that's not pleasant."

A tear had slipped out of Mo's eye, and Val wiped it away with a tissue. "I'm sorry, honey," Val whispered in her ear. "It's over—let's get you out of here."

"Is there anything she's supposed to do or not do?" Val asked.

"She should take it easy today and really as much as possible."

Val wrote: Dr. Sheldon says she shouldn't be having any procedures or appointments in the next week or two. She needs to rest and let her fractures heal. Her bones really need more Vitamin D. She needs some sun.

Goldie opened the front passenger door for Mo. "Mo, dear, you sit up here. Let me help you in. You've been crying. Oh, I'm so sorry."

After Mo was settled in the front seat, Val checked her phone. Missed call from Julie. Missed call and voice mail from Sophie.

"I cannot put off Julie anymore," Val said, starting the car. She put her phone on speaker and tapped on Julie's number.

Julie answered on the first ring. "Hi, Val. I've been trying to reach you for days. Are you all right?"

"Yes, thank you. I'm sorry—I had family in town. I haven't seen Lily in a couple of days. Is she okay?"

"I suppose. I just wanted to ask you about something. One of my friends was at Wildwood Shopping Center last week. Actually, it was the day you had Mom out, and she missed her PT appointment. Anyway, she said she saw Mom walking by herself. Then she said she saw a tall woman come running up to her. She said it looked like Mom was lost. Is that true?"

"Well, we were at Wildwood. We stopped there for a few minutes after Lily saw Dr. Banford. We had a lovely time window-shopping. I know I was excited about something in that Pink Store, and I made Lily look at it, but I was with her the whole time. I'm not sure what your friend is referring to. Maybe it was someone else."

"I don't think so. She knows Mom."

"Well, I'm not sure what to tell you, Julie. We went to Dr. Banford's, stopped by Wildwood to pick up some prescriptions, and we did a little window-shopping before we went to the park. I think I told you that Dr. Banford said Lily needs a little sun because her Vitamin D is low. I was with her the whole time. It was a very nice day, actually."

Silence.

Val's phone rang—Sophie.

"I'm sorry, Julie, but I have another call. I'm sorry if you were worried about her. She was absolutely fine. I'll plan on taking her this week if that's all right with you. I'd like to see her. Bye."

"I think there's something wrong with Sophie," Val said. She turned the speaker off and put her phone up to her ear.

"Are you okay?"

"No, I'm not okay. Don't you listen to your messages anymore? I—"

"I was with Mo at her appointments. I was just about—"

"Well, now you've gone and done it." Sophie was crying. "I told you I didn't want that CT scan. I didn't want to know. I don't care! Now—"

"Whoa, hold on a minute." Val pulled the car over onto the shoulder. "Why don't you start from the beginning?"

"I don't know," she said, sobbing. "I wasn't listening. Some blood vessel in my head that I could've told them. Roz is hysterical. She already has all these other appointments lined up. I'm supposed to stay in my bed. God forbid my head blows up and I die."

"What do you mean? You have an aneurysm?"

"I told you! I don't know! I don't care! Out of here, Val. You said out of here. If you don't get me out here, I'm getting out myself. You can deal with Roz."

Sophie hung up.

Val put her phone down and shut her eyes.

"What's the matter?" Goldie asked.

"Sophie is upset. I think she has an aneurysm."

"Oh no," Mo said. "Can they fix it?"

Val shrugged. "I don't know. I'm not sure it really matters."

She called Sophie back.

"What?"

"We'll be there in fifteen minutes. Don't go anywhere."

GOLDIE

"Hi, dear. How are you?"

"Rotten," Goldie said, sliding into the front seat.

"What's up? You were good yesterday."

"My lease is up next month, and David says I *have* to move in with him. They can't afford to do anything else."

"Hmm. How much is it?'

"Three thousand a month."

"Hmm. Well, I can cover you for a while until you decide what you really want to do."

"Oh, you're so sweet. It's okay. I'll figure it out."

"You will? You have options?"

"A woman always has options, honey. Don't you think?"

"Umm, I suppose. You could be homeless, I guess."

"Well, I'm not going to worry about it right now."

"Okay. Well, I'm here if you need me. Where are we going? Kravitz's?"

"No." Goldie took out a piece of paper from her purse. "Deborah Sussman. Five five three zero Wisconsin."

Val looked at her. "You're changing doctors?"

"I think so. One of my friends saw her and loved her. Besides, all my doctors are old as dirt. Maybe it's time for a fresh look at things."

"I suppose. It's just so hard starting with someone new."

Goldie shrugged. "Things change."

They stopped in the lobby to check the directory. Val found Dr. Deborah Sussman and then leaned closer to make sure she had read it correctly: Gynecology and Gynecologic Surgery.

She looked at Goldie. "Oh. I thought you were seeing an internist."

"No. I'm fit as a fiddle. I haven't been to my gynecologist in a while, though. And as I said, he's starting to grow moss."

"Oh. Okay."

Goldie was quick with her paperwork. Ten minutes later a young woman in an apricot scrub shirt and white pants opened the door to the back office and called her name.

"Goldie, why don't you leave your purse here with me? No sense taking any chances."

Goldie hesitated and then handed over her purse. "I didn't steal anything, so you're safe with it."

"Oh, don't be silly. It's just a new office and…you just never know these days."

Val watched her go through the door and looked at her purse. Options? she thought. Are you kidding, Goldie? Or are you lying? She stood and went to the bathroom in the hall. She went in a stall and sat down on the closed toilet seat. She opened Goldie's purse looking for her phone, but the first things she saw were two bank envelopes. One was open—hundred dollar bills. The other—an inch thick—was sealed. She found Goldie's phone in the bottom, took it out, tapped on it. Then for several seconds, she just stared at it, digesting the fact that it was now password protected.

Fighting off a sudden irritation, she quickly smiled. Goldie was just full of surprises.

For almost a minute, she just sat there, staring at the phone. Okay, she finally said to herself. Four numbers. Four numbers that were familiar, that Goldie could remember. Four numbers that were important to her. Birthday—0425—nope. 0437—nope. 1937—nope. She took out Sophie's wallet—last four of social security—5692—nope. Last four of cell phone—2940—nope. House phone—nope.

For another minute she stayed still on the toilet, staring at the row of four blank white boxes. Then she took out her own phone and pulled up the calendar. Four numbers. Four numbers that Goldie could remember. Four numbers that were important to her. 0823—nope. But, no, it was actually early the next morning that Frank had died—ten or fifteen minutes past midnight. 0824—bingo.

Tap—recent phone calls: Saul, Saul, Saul, Saul, David, Saul, Val, Saul, Saul.

Tap—voice mail: Saul, Saul, Saul, Val, Saul.

Tap—text messages: Saul, Val.

Tap on Saul. Scroll up ten messages:

Saul: What about this weekend?
Goldie: That would be great.
Saul: I'll stay downtown. I can pick u up.
Goldie: Let's talk about it. I have to figure out David.
Saul: Okay. I miss u. Can't wait.
Goldie: I miss u too. It's been too long.
Saul: Pls think about what we talked about.
Goldie: I will. Promise. Val's here.
Saul: Okay. Call me.
Goldie: Doctor appt at 10. Call u after. Heart icon.

Val closed her eyes, opened them.

Tap again to voice mail. Val looked at the names, looked at her watch. She tapped Saul's latest message, started to listen, then felt a sudden wave of guilt as if she were listening through a closed door. She stopped the message, put the phone back, closed her eyes again.

Suddenly she opened them. She checked Saul's area code again—239. She took her own phone and tapped in a search for area code 239—Naples, Florida.

Naples. Florida. Goldie's "best friend" lived in Florida. In Naples, if she remembered correctly. Rhonda, if she remembered correctly. Rhonda, whom Goldie had been visiting twice a year ever since Val had known her. Twice a year by herself. Rhonda. Naples. Florida. Saul.

Goldie. *Really*, Goldie? Rhonda?

Goldie came out of the back office holding onto several pieces of paper. Val stood and handed her purse to her. Goldie folded the papers, put them in her purse, took her phone out. On the way to the elevator, she checked it and then put it away.

They were quiet in the elevator, quiet on the way to the car.

"Well, did you like her?" Val finally asked.

"Yes, I did. She's very different than Dr. Goldberg."

"How so? Just because she's a woman?"

Goldie was quiet for a moment. "I suppose that's part of it. I don't know. We actually talked about stuff. I mean real stuff. I think I spent more time talking about Frank with Dr. Goldberg then I did talking about me."

In the car, Val said, "Are you okay? It looks like she gave you some prescriptions."

"I'm fine, thanks. Just girl stuff."

"Do you want to get them filled? We can go to Starbucks and wait for them."

"Sure. That sounds good."

Goldie took out her phone, tapped on it, tapped again, put it away.

"Goldie, I was thinking while you were with the doctor, why don't you get out of here for a few days if David is being difficult?

Maybe you could go see your friend in Florida. What's her name? Rhonda?"

"Funny you say that," Goldie said, looking at her purse. "I just talked to her yesterday. She might come up here actually. Maybe even this weekend."

Val looked straight ahead as she visualized Goldie's recent calls. There weren't any from Rhonda, or if there had been, they'd been deleted. But that didn't make sense. Why would she delete Rhonda's calls and not Saul's? Because she didn't. And if she was such a good friend, why wasn't she at Frank's service?

"That would be a good break," Val said. "Maybe I can meet her. I'm surprised I didn't meet her at Frank's service. Was she there?"

"No, she couldn't make it. She had some family thing she had to do."

"That's too bad. Well, maybe I can meet her this weekend."

"I hope so," Goldie said, looking out the window. "You'd like her. Yes, I think you would."

⊨⊹ ⊹⊨

Val dropped Goldie in front of the pharmacy and went into Starbucks. Goldie arrived fifteen minutes later.

"Were they busy?" Val asked.

"No, I stopped by the bank. Sorry."

Val pictured the stack of hundred dollar bills that Goldie had pulled out in Victoria's Secret. Two or three thousand, she figured. And the other two wads in her purse. "Do you need some money? I'm happy to help."

"No, I'm fine for now. Thanks, though. I just wanted to put some things in my safe deposit box before David starts going through my place."

"I see. Well, just let me know if I can help."

Goldie got a cappuccino and sat down. "So, you're serious about this trip, aren't you?"

"Dead serious. Mo's headed downhill in a hurry, Sophie's got an aneurysm that's probably inoperable, and Lily doesn't know where she is half the time. It's now or never."

Goldie nodded. "You think you can handle it all?"

Val shrugged. "I'll get help. I've already looked into visiting nurses in Georgia. And if I can't—if we can't—then we'll come home."

"It's all very nice of you. I hope it works out."

Val shrugged again. "It will work out, one way or another. So where do you want to go?"

"Florida, I guess. I don't know where else I'd go."

"To see Rhonda? That's the one place you'd want to go?"

Goldie thought for a moment. "Yes, yes, it is. I like it there."

"Do you ever think about moving? You have Rhonda, and I'm sure you'd make a lot of other friends pretty quickly."

Goldie slowly stirred her cappuccino. "I've been thinking about it. It would be hard to leave you all, but I think I'd be okay otherwise."

"Well, as they say, you only live once."

"Isn't that right."

"If you move in with David, getting away might be harder down the road."

Still swirling, Goldie nodded. Her phone rang—the pharmacy—her prescriptions were ready.

LILY

"And Val, I know you won't, but please don't leave her alone."

"Of course not, Julie. Not for a second."

"I've tried every which way to reschedule this closing, but the buyers *have* to close today."

"I understand. It's really not a problem, Julie. I enjoy having the time with Lily. And I'll write down everything for you."

"That would be a big help."

"And more," Val said under her breath, ending the call. She was parked in the fire lane in the front driveway of the Towers Assisted Living Facility. "Okay, girls." She glanced at Goldie in the front seat and then turned and looked at Sophie in the back seat. "Anyone want to come up?"

"Depends. Are there any new men up there?" Sophie asked.

"None that don't drool," Val said.

"I'll pass," Goldie said.

"I'll pass," Sophie said. "And don't have brunch like you usually do. I got diabetes, you know. And an aneurysm. I need breakfast."

"You had breakfast. I saw it. I'll just be a few minutes. Don't go anywhere."

"That was a snack. I got diabetes, Val," Sophie called after her through the open car window. "I'm not kidding. And I'm feeling a little faint." Whoosh, whoosh. "And I need some coffee."

Val shook her head and disappeared through the door.

"Good morning, Mrs. Kantor," Petra said. "Mrs. Preston is at her table. Do you want me to get her?"

"I'll get her, Petra. Thank you."

Lily was by herself looking out the window, her hands folded in her lap. Val sat down across from her and waited for her to turn.

"Lily, honey," she said after a moment.

Lily turned to look at her, her eyes gray and lifeless for a moment. Then they flickered in recognition, and she put out her hand. "Well, good morning, Val. What a surprise. I'm so delighted to see you."

Val took her hand between hers. "Good morning, Lily. How are you?" Lily's hand was bony and frail, her skin warm, as if Val were holding a small bird. Her white blouse was freshly dry cleaned, but there were specks of coffee down her sleeve and a small smear of marmalade on her cuff.

"I'm well, thank you."

Lily looked at Val, somewhat nervously, Val thought.

"Are you ready for your appointment, honey? Remember, we're going to see that new doctor today."

"Yes, I do remember, dear. You are so kind to take me."

"My pleasure." Val helped Lily up from her chair. "We have to stop by your room for a minute and make a quick call. Then we're out of here. Goldie and Sophie are waiting in the car, and we're going to pick up Mo after your appointment. We're going to play cards in the park."

"Who, dear? I'm sorry, I don't think I heard you."

"Goldie and Sophie."

"Oh, yes. How fun. I don't think I've played cards in ages."

Val took her arm and headed toward Lily's room. "Come on, let's go before we get old," she whispered in her ear.

"Oh, let's go right now, dear. I do not want to get old."

Halfway across the dining room, Lily stopped next to a table of octo- and nonagenarians. "Frank—Friday," she said.

"I'm sorry, Lily. What was that?"

"Frank—Friday," she said, smiling proudly. "Frank—Friday."

<hr />

"Well, if it isn't Miss Georgia Peach," Sophie said, sliding over in the seat. "Where the heck have you been?"

Lily looked to Val and then Sophie. "Why, dear, I was at a funeral with you."

Sophie looked at her with surprise. "Damn right you were. And we had to take a damn cab home."

"Yes, I do remember you brought me home. In a taxi if I remember correctly."

"Yeah, forty-two damn bucks. And Val only gave me forty."

"Hi, Lily," Goldie said. "Thank you so much for coming to Frank's service. It really meant a lot to me."

"Oh, my…"

"Goldie," Val finished. "Lily wouldn't have missed it for anything."

"Well, we still missed half of it," Sophie said. "Someone I know can't hold her liquor."

"Okay, Sophie, enough. Do you two still want to go to Starbucks while we go to the doctor?"

"Well, I sure as poo-poo don't want to go to the neurologist's again. Can I borrow some money, Val?"

"I've got money," Goldie said, looking at her phone.

"I guess so if you're spending three hundred bucks on underwear. Can you lend me some?"

"My treat," Goldie said. Tap, tap, tap.

Val glanced at her. "So, Goldie, you said Rhonda might come up for the weekend. Is she going to come? Are we going to get to meet her?"

"I'm talking to her now, actually. I think she is going to come. She might have a tight schedule, though. She has relatives she has to see in Virginia."

"Maybe we can have a quick lunch."

"I'll ask her. That would be nice."

"Where is she going to stay?"

"Downtown, I think. Don't ask me why, but she likes it there."

"Oh. Well, that's nice. Hopefully we can have lunch."

"Is she on the prowl, too?" Sophie said.

"Stop it, Sophie." Val flashed her an irritated look.

Goldie was still looking at her phone. "I'm sitting shiva, Sophie. How many times do I have to tell you?"

"Okay, girls," Val said, pulling up to the front of Starbucks. "No trouble. I'm running out of excuses."

The Center for Cognitive Disorders was on the seventh floor. Val helped Lily fill out her paperwork, and then Lily was whisked away alone. The only way to properly evaluate her, the woman in the plum scrub suit and white lab coat had said. It would take about forty-five minutes.

Val sat for a few minutes pondering her options. She sent Goldie a text asking if they were okay. She listened to all of her old voice mails. She checked her e-mail. She looked at her watch. Finally, she stood and asked the receptionist for a clipboard and some blank paper.

Back in her chair, she took her new iPad mini out of her purse and went to the Internet. Winnebagos, she typed in. Then: de luxe, handicapped access, rental. Within seconds her screen was populated with websites and ads. She set the iPad in her lap with the clipboard, went into the first website, started to write.

The plum woman had to call her name twice before she heard her. When they were in the back office, she said, "Dr. Woolschlager would like to talk to you first and then you and Mrs. Preston together. Is her daughter coming?"

"She's in a closing," Val said. "It's okay. I go to most of Lily's appointments with her and go over them with Julie."

Dr. Woolschlager shook her hand and gave her a chair across from his desk. "You are a close family friend, I gather?"

"Yes. I've been very close to Lily for a long time. And Julie."

He nodded. "I spoke with Julie a little while ago. I'm not sure she's going to make it."

"It's okay. I'm going to write everything down." Val poised the clipboard on her lap and looked at the doctor expectantly.

Dr. Woolschlager scratched his nose for a moment. "Apparently Mrs. Preston's son is coming." He looked at his watch. "He called his sister to get directions. He should be here any minute."

"Her son?" Val said, trying to act surprised. "Walker?"

"Yes, I think she said Walker." He scratched his nose again. "She, uh, she didn't seem too happy about it. I guess Mrs. Preston called him earlier today."

"That's interesting."

Doctor Woolschlager gave a little shrug and opened his hands.

Val looked at her watch. "Okay. Well, do you want to wait for him?"

The doctor looked at his watch.

"We can start, and I'll fill him in, too," Val volunteered.

"I think that's probably best. Well," he said after a moment, "sometimes we don't like to put exact labels on these problems. In the long run whether we say Mrs. Preston has Alzheimer's disease or some other cognitive disorder, the exact label really doesn't matter so much. Maybe a little for the medication I'm going to recommend, but not really otherwise. The reality is that she does have a cognitive disorder, which I suspect is worsening, at least according to her daughter. Our testing would support that as well. Do you see that as her friend?"

Val wrote: Lily has a small component of a cognitive disorder. She primarily is socially isolated.

"Honestly, no, I'm not sure I do, Doctor. She's quiet when she's at the Towers because she doesn't have many people to talk to. When she's out with her friends, she's as lively as ever. She's a wonderful bridge player."

Dr. Woolschlager frowned. "That's probably not what I would have expected, but sometimes good friends can bring out a certain capacity."

Val wrote: The most stimulating activity that Lily can do now is be out with her friends. Playing cards is an excellent way to stimulate her mental faculties. She needs to do it as much as she can.

"I think that's probably true," Val said when she was finished writing. "All I can say is she's sharp as a whip when her friends are around."

He nodded. "Well, the real question is whether Mrs. Preston is able to stay in her current living situation. Her daughter is of the mind that she probably needs to move to a specialized cognitive disorder facility."

Val pursed her lips. "You're obviously the expert, Doctor, but I'm just wondering if moving her to a place where she'll have even fewer people to talk to is the best thing for her."

"Well, I understand your point, but these facilities have a lot of structured programs. And I'm not saying it has to be done next week. I do think it's on the horizon fairly soon, though."

Val wrote: The doctor thinks Lily needs more social interaction. She may need to move in a year or two, but for now she just needs to get out more.

The plum nurse opened the office door. "Mrs. Preston's son is here," she said. "Do you want me to bring him in?"

Dr. Woolschlager looked at his watch again.

"I'll fill Walker in on everything," Val said. "Are we going to meet with Lily together?"

"Yes, I think that's a good idea. Let me speak with her, and then we'll all sit for a few minutes."

Dr. Woolschlager walked out. A moment later the door opened again, and the nurse showed Walker in.

Val looked at her watch, looked at Walker, raised her eyebrows.

Walker had a tie on but no jacket. His tie was loose at the knot exposing the top button of his shirt, which was unbuttoned. He was fair like Lily, but his face was freckled and patchy from the sun. Little beads of sweat dotted his forehead, and his cheeks were flushed.

"I'm sorry, Val. I, uh, I had a little trouble finding this place."

"Lily gave you directions on the phone. I know, because I wrote them down for her."

"I, uh, I wrote them down, but then I couldn't find them. I didn't want to bother you if you were already, so I had to call Julie."

Val thought she smelled alcohol. Val knew she smelled alcohol. She nodded and looked at her watch again.

"Did you have a nice brunch, Walker?"

Walker looked at the floor and looked up. "Yes, ma'am."

"Where did you eat? At the corner bar?"

Walker didn't answer.

Val studied him for a moment. "I'll tell you what, Walker," she said. "It was very nice of Lily to call you, but you are a little late. I'll make you a deal. I won't tell Julie that you were late and that you smell like a distillery, and you let me tell her and you about this appointment."

"Yes, ma'am."

The door opened. A nurse walked Lily in and said the doctor would be there in a minute. Walker stood, hesitated, then moved to hug his mother.

"Walker," Val said when he let go of his mother.

"Yes, ma'am."

"One more thing."

Walker looked down at the floor. Val was sure there were tears in his eyes.

"I think it would be a really good idea for you to spend some time with your mother soon. I think you should go away with her for a few days."

Walker looked up, the sweat on his forehead glistening in the light.

"You need to call Julie in the next few days and tell her. I'll tell you when." Walker, looking like he was about to vomit, nodded.

"You need to be firm, Walker—Lily is your mother, too. Right, Lily?"

"Why, yes, Val. Of course."

"I'll help you with it, Walker. And try not to look so happy. She's your mother."

Dr. Woolschlager came through the door, stopped, looked from Val to Walker and back. "Is everything okay?"

"Yes, just fine," Val said. "Walker and I haven't seen each other for a while, and we were just catching up."

Dr. Woolschlager helped Lily to a chair and moved around his desk.

"Sit down, Walker," Val said. "It'll be okay."

⊯ ⊯

Mo picked the game—five card stud, nothing wild. They were sitting at their favorite picnic table in the shade of a large stately elm tree. Val had her iPad out and was glancing at it as she played.

"King bed or queen bed?" she said, drawing a card. "I'm going to get hotel rooms, but just in case we need to sleep in it."

"Ask Miss Victoria," Sophie said.

"Stop it, Sophie. I don't think we can get three people in a king, so the queen's probably fine. Mo and maybe Lily could sleep in that. There's a double pull-out in the main cabin that will sleep two. Goldie and Sophie could sleep there. And there's a couch. I'll be fine on the couch."

"You can't sleep on a couch," Goldie said. "Particularly if you're paying for it."

"I'll be fine. We shouldn't have to sleep in it anyway."

"What if Vicky does get lucky and needs the bedroom?" Sophie asked, studying her cards. "Then what do we do? I'm not into threesomes."

"I'm still in mourning, Sophie. Remember? You're the one who has ants in her pants."

Sophie made a noise and took a card. "I'm out. Where's my luck today? Maybe it's that thing in my brain. Maybe I'm confused."

"Oh, don't say that, Sophie," Mo said, looking intently at her cards.

"You and Roz," Sophie said. "It is what it is."

"Until it isn't," Goldie said.

"Oh, that's good," Sophie said. "I have to remember that one."

"Lily," Val said softly.

Lily looked up from her cards.

"Do you want a card, honey?"

Lily looked back. "No, Miss Val, I'm just fine."

"Come on, Mo," Sophie said. "Make her show us what she's got. Let's see if Miss Georgia Peach is bluffing again."

Mo slid a quarter into the center of the table. "What'cha got, Lily? Can you beat two pairs?" Mo turned over a pair of eights and Jacks.

"Lily?" Val said. "Do you have anything, or are you just taking our quarters again?"

Lily looked at her cards and frowned.

Val leaned over. "Let me help you, honey. Oh, you were just bluffing us again, you silly-willy." Val took the quarters and pushed them over to Mo. "Today's your day, Mo."

Mo raked in the quarters, grimaced, adjusted herself on the bench.

"Are you okay?" Val asked. "Just let me know when you want to go home. Mary Catherine's probably expecting you soon. I told her we were only taking you out for a little while."

"Yeah, Mo," Sophie said. "You don't want to worry Mom."

Mo moved around some more and looked at her watch. "It's five o'clock somewhere," she said brightly. "How about a glass of wine before I go home, Val? She'll be in her office for a while."

"Oh my," Lily said. "Is it really five o'clock?"

"Yeah, in Greenland," Sophie said. "But that's close enough. Come on, Val. Just one glass."

Val looked at her watch—3:00 p.m. "I don't know, girls. It's a little early."

"For who?" Sophie said. "What else are we going to do?"

"Plan our trip. Mo, you haven't really said where you want to go. Have you thought about it?"

"Don't answer her, Mo," Sophie said. "Hold out until she cracks."

Mo passed the deck to Sophie, trying not to look at Val.

"Blackjack," Sophie said.

"Oh, all right," Val said, reaching for her soft cooler. "Just one though—it's early." She pulled out a bottle of chardonnay that she had already opened and five Styrofoam cups.

"Cakebread," Sophie said. "Wow. Thanks, Val. You ever had Cakebread, Mo?"

"I don't believe so."

"It's a hundred bucks a bottle in a restaurant."

"That's right, girls." Val poured four glasses of wine and water for Lily. "Nothing but the best. Cheers."

Sophie took a long sip. "Oh, that is good." She swirled the wine in her cup and took another. "Are you sure you can drive that thing, Val?"

"You're darn right I can. I drove a bus in the air force for a while. So where would you like to go, Mo? Lily wants to go to Sea Island. Goldie said she'd probably like to go to Florida. I'm still trying to decide."

"And what am I, chopped liver?"

"You said you don't care—you just want out."

"Well, maybe I changed my mind. I'm thinking about Vegas. How about Vegas, Mo? We can play cards and drink wine twenty-four seven."

"I just don't know if I can do a trip," Mo said softly.

"The Winnebago will have everything you need, Mo," Val said. "And we'll help you."

"Of course we'll help you, Mo," Goldie said. "You have to go with us."

"Twenty-four seven, Mo. Think about it."

Mo's lower lip was starting to quiver. "It's not just that. I don't think Mary Catherine will let me go. And I...it's been so long since I've been away."

"Val will take care of Mary Catherine, Mo. Don't worry about that."

Mo bit her lip.

"You're going to Mass on Sunday, aren't you?" Val asked.

Mo nodded.

"Why don't you talk to Father Kelly about it? That might make you feel better."

Mo seemed to brighten. "I do need to speak with him," she said. "You know, about that other little thing."

"What other thing?" Sophie asked. "Are you on probation now, too?"

Mo looked to Val.

"No," Val said. "It was nothing. Just a prescription thing. Hit me, please."

Sophie looked at the both of them quizzically. "'A prescription thing'?"

"A doctor thing. It was nothing." Val tapped her down card with her forefinger. "Hit me, please."

Sophie dealt her a card faceup. Val looked at the ace, back to Sophie, smiled. "You feeling lucky now, sweetness?"

Sophie looked back at her and held her gaze. "Very," she said, turning over a card without looking at it. "I think you're bluffing."

VAL

Val turned in her bed and reached for Jules. Her hand moved slowly over the long pillow beside her, searching for his muscular arm, his shoulder, the thick muscles of his neck. She found his arm, ran her hand up and down it, the hair softer there, then across his chest, the hair coarser and thicker. She tried to pull him closer to her, but he was still, immovable. She inched herself closer, pulling herself up against him, searching for his warm breaths, then his beard as she ran her hand over his cheek. She put her arm around his back, draped her leg over his thigh, pulled herself even closer.

Something was wrong, though, and she stirred in her bed, almost woke in the predawn light. She ran her hand down his leg, feeling the large bone in his thigh where there used to be muscle and then back up and over the bone in his arm and then the skin of his cheek. She moved almost on top of him, curling her arm around his back, pulling him in, pulling him away from the cancer eating him up from the inside out. She put her hand on his chin, tilted his face toward her, put her lips on his. They were firm, cold, unyielding. Terrified, she moved her head back and tried to cry aloud, but no sounds or words would come. Her heart jumped. Literally.

Thump, skip, thump, skip, skip, thump, thump, thump.

She woke abruptly, and for a moment, her arm still curled around the pillow, she still felt him beside her. And then, the light slipping into the room, the thumping in her chest demanding her attention, he was gone.

She closed her eyes, opened them, closed them again. Gone. Gone, gone, gone. Gone again, until the day was done and the night could wrap its arms around the two of them.

Thump, skip, thump, thump, thump. Painful now, incessant now. She realized she'd forgotten to take her pills before she'd gone to bed, and she reached for the bottles and the water on the nightstand. Falling back on her pillow she stayed still, waiting for the wild piece of muscle in her chest to calm.

Finally, after several minutes, she could breathe without an effort. She looked at her phone—6:05 a.m. No new messages, no new e-mails. Too early to make any calls. She pulled her iPad off the nightstand and checked the weather forecast. Then she went to the Internet and the websites she had saved from the day before.

Thump, skip, thump, thump, thump...

Eastern RV Enterprises Inc. opened at 8:00 a.m. Moving around her kitchen with her phone on speaker and her iPad glowing on the kitchen island, Val called at 8:01 a.m.

"Ralph, this is Val Kantor. We spoke yesterday afternoon about a Winnebago rental. You were going to look into it for me."

"Yep. I got it all right here. You decide about round trip or one way yet?"

"Umm, one way, I think." Val had a row of pill bottles lined up on the black granite island, and she was studying their labels as she spoke. "We'll probably fly back."

"Where are you planning to drop it off?"

"Umm, Florida or Nevada. I'm not sure yet. Can I tell you later?" She took out a box of plastic sandwich bags, a black pen, and set them on the island in front of the pill bottles.

"Florida or Nevada? Is that what you said? They're a little far apart, you know."

"Yes, Ralph. I am aware of that."

"Okay. It's your dollar. You can return it wherever you want as long as we have a dealer in that city. We do in Vegas. Depends on where you're going in Florida. We have dealers in most of the bigger towns. They're listed on the website."

"One way then. I'll make it work." She took a pill bottle that was labeled with her name and emptied a pile of little orange tablets onto the glistening island.

"Okay. It's more expensive one way, though. You know that, right?"

"That's okay."

"You'll be the only driver?"

"Yes, just me." She took a bottle labeled Maureen Flanagan and emptied the same type of orange pills into the pile of her pills.

"Are you aware that your regular car insurance doesn't cover a 'Bago like this? We can provide you the insurance."

"That's fine." She took a sandwich bag, opened it below the edge of the island, swept the pile of pills into the bag. Xanax, she wrote on the bag.

"What about twenty-four-seven roadside assistance? You want that? It's probably a good idea unless you have a mechanic with you. It's a two-ton 'Bago. It ain't something you can put up on a jack."

"Yes, of course." She emptied another bottle of pills that was labeled with her name and then the other bottle of pills with Mo's name.

"Okay. I wish everyone was like you. So, let me see here. We got a 'Bago Journey, pick-up in Frederick, Maryland, drop off in Florida or Vegas. Three thousand a week plus insurance and road-side and you want it for a month. Is that right?"

"That's right," she said, sweeping the pile of pills into a plastic bag.

"The insurance is twelve hundred for the month and the road-side is four hundred."

"Okay." Sonata, she wrote.

"What do you want to use for the deposit?"

"American Express, but can I just double-check a couple of things with you first?"

"Sure."

"There's a queen in the bedroom and a double pull-out in the sitting area?"

"Yep. And another couch that someone could sleep on. Two would be tough on that."

"One is fine. Wheelchair access?"

"Well, not technically, but there are air-lift steps."

Val paused. "That will be okay, I think. Flat screen TVs?"

"Three. Up front, the living room, and the bedroom. They all have satellite or cable access."

"There's a table in the living area that's big enough for five of us to play cards?"

"It's built for cards."

"And a refrigerator that will hold wine bottles."

"It's a full refrigerator and freezer."

"Okay. You want my card number?" She emptied the last bottle of pills on the island and swept them into a bag.

"Sounds like a fun trip. Wish I could go."

"How old are you?" Vicodin, she wrote on the label.

"Fifty-five."

"Umm, I'm not sure you'd fit in. Maybe next time."

⇥ ⇤

"I thought you just wanted to draw my blood again. We did this the other day."

Dr. Harold Bernstein took his stethoscope out of his ears, moved his glasses down his nose, peered at her over the rims. "We do—your calcium is low. But I haven't seen your EKG, and you don't look so hot. You got it done, didn't you?"

"I'm going to do it this afternoon. Along with all the other things I'm supposed to do."

"Val, this is serious business." He put the stethoscope back in his ears, back on her chest, and moved it around emphatically. "You're still arrhythmic. Maybe even more than the other day. Are you taking your meds?"

"Of course I'm taking my meds, Harold. Why would you even ask that?"

"Because you didn't get your EKG done, your rhythm is worse, and I think you're depressed."

"Don't worry—I won't keel over on your shift."

"You will if you keep procrastinating. And I'm serious about the meds, particularly the beta-blocker. It's controlling your rate, which is already high. If you don't take it, your rate is going to go through the roof and your heart can't handle that."

"Hmm. I guess that's better than down into the Beltway."

"That's not funny, Val."

"I guess not. I'll get it done this afternoon, Harold. Promise."

"Tell them to fax it to me or e-mail it. I'll call you about that and your calcium. I don't know why that's low, but it needs to come up. Are you taking your supplement?"

"Yes, Harold."

"Don't forget the Vitamin D."

Val buttoned her shirt and tucked it into her skirt. "And then what?"

"And then what, what?"

"If you don't like my EKG. Then what?"

"We'll have to see. It's possible I can just adjust your meds. If you're missing too many beats, though, we might need to talk about putting in a pacemaker."

Val nodded, picked up her purse, headed for the door.

"By the way," Dr. Bernstein added, "Bill called me yesterday. They're concerned about you keeping your appointments. They think you spend too much time on your friends and not enough on yourself."

"'They'?"

"Debbie and Roger, too, I guess. I didn't ask."

"And 'they' asked you to talk to me, so you're talking to me?"

"More or less."

"Call my cell, Harold. I'll be out. With my friends."

⇒+ +⇐

Goldie called at nine-thirty.

"The mall doesn't open until ten," Val said.

"I know. I just want to get out of here."

"I'm just leaving Bernstein's. I'll be there in about ten or fifteen minutes."

"I'll be out front. I have some Starbucks gift cards."

"Oh, that's nice. Where'd you get them?"

"Rhonda sent them to me. She gets them with her Amex points."

"That's nice of her. Is she excited about coming up?"

"Yeah, she needs a break, too. I don't know why. It's beautiful down there."

"Okay. I'll see you in a few."

Rhonda, Saul. Rhonda. Rhonda who called but didn't. New gynecologist. Hmm. What else was up with Miss Victoria's Secret?

The direct number to the CVS pharmacy next to Starbucks was stored in Val's phone. She knew the main pharmacist, but she didn't think she'd have to speak to her.

"Hi," she said, adjusting the volume on her earpiece. "This is Maggie from Dr. Kravitz's office. I don't think I need to speak to the pharmacist. One of our patients, Goldie Tannenbaum, got some prescriptions the other day from another doctor, and Dr. Kravitz just wants to double-check the dosages. She's in the office now, but she doesn't remember exactly...Sure, I can hold... Vagifem ten micrograms and Viagra fifty milligrams. Okay, thank you, that's a big help."

Val smiled and shook her head. "Girl stuff," she said to herself. Goldie—*really?*

Her phone rang—St. Patrick's rectory.

"Hello, Father Kelly...thank you so much for calling me back. I know you're very busy...I was calling about Maureen Flanagan. We call her Mo. Anyway, as I think you know, I'm a very close friend of hers. In fact, I was with her at Mass the other day when she had Reconciliation with you. Anyway, I'm little worried about her, and sometimes it's uh—how should I put it—maybe a little hard with Mary Catherine because she loves her so much and she's very protective...Yes, you're right, maybe a little overprotective. Anyway, I'm a little worried, and I was hoping you had a minute to talk...I think she's going to talk to you about this on Sunday. In a nutshell, as you know, she's having a lot of medical problems. Several of her doctors would like to see her get away for a few days. Her Vitamin D is low, and she could actually use a little sun. I think she's worried about bringing it up with Mary Catherine, though. She knows how Mary Catherine feels so responsible for everything, and Mo doesn't want to upset her. I'm pretty sure Mo would actually like to get away, but she's just feeling guilty about it...That's very nice, Father. She trusts you more than anyone...Thank you, again...Yes, we'll try to have some fun. Thank you."

Goldie was sitting on a bench outside her condominium entrance looking at her phone. Seeing Val, she dropped it in her purse and almost jumped into the car. "Oh my gosh. I have so many things I have to do before Rhonda comes. Thank God I'm getting my car back."

"I can help you. Is your car ready? Do you want to go get it?"

"No, then I'll have to pay for it. Let David take me later."

"So what do you have to do?"

"I need to get some things at the mall. Then if we're really going away, I have to get back into my safe deposit box. And at some point, I have to stop by my lawyer's office."

"Well, we really are going away, so where do you want to start?"

Goldie looked at her watch. "The mall. I need some nightgowns. All my things are a hundred years old.

"Macy's has some nice things. I think they're on sale, too."

Goldie looked at her as if she were kidding. "Val, dear. Vicky's please. I've been looking online. I think I know just what I want."

Val turned out and headed toward the mall. "Let me guess—black. See-through."

"Black or red. The red looked cute, too. Maybe both."

"Hmm," Val said. "I think I need to meet this Rhonda."

THREE

To die will be an awfully big adventure.

Aristotle

LILY

"Mom?" Walker said after a moment, sounding as if his doctor had just told him he was about to have a rectal exam.

"Walker, why it's so nice to hear your voice."

"Mom? Uh, are you all right?"

Val wrote quickly on the notepad in front of Lily.

"Why, yes, of course, honey. I'm just fine."

"Uh, that's good, Mom. Uh, it was nice to see you the other day. I'm sorry I was late."

Lily looked at the pad. "That's okay, dear. I know you're very busy at work." Val wrote on the pad again and held it up for her. "Val reminded me that you had a wonderful idea about just the two of us going away together. That's so sweet of you."

"Uh, yeah, I...uh, I thought it would be nice for us. I can't hear you very well, Mom. Where are you?"

Lily looked at Val; Val wrote as fast as she could in big block letters.

"I'm in my room, dear," Lily answered. "My phone is on speaker. I don't know why, but I hear better that way."

"Oh."

"Do you have some place in mind, dear?"

"Uh, for what, Mom?"

"To go away, dear. Just the two of us."

"Uh, not really. Is there some place you'd like to go?"

"Well, I have been thinking about it. I'd really like to go to Sea Island for a few days. You know, that's where your father and I went on our honeymoon."

"Sea Island? You mean in Georgia?"

"Yes, dear. I do believe it's in Georgia."

"Uh, okay. I can look into that, I guess."

"I think we should go soon, honey. Can you get away next week?" Lily moved closer to the pad. "That's our anniversary, you know."

"Next week?" Walker said, his voice squeaky and strained as if his doctor's finger were now squarely on his prostate gland. "Uh, I can try, Mom. It's kind of short notice at work."

Lily peered at the pad and smiled. "I'll get sick if you want. You know, so you have an excuse."

Silence.

"That's okay—I think I can get off. Uh, Mom, uh…does Julie know about this?"

"Why, dear, I don't know. I thought you had talked to her."

"Umm, not yet."

"Well, I'd really like to spend some time alone with you. I see her quite a bit. Maybe you should let her know, honey. Otherwise she'll worry her head off."

"Yes, you're right."

"You call her when you have a chance, honey."

"Okay, Mom."

"Bye, dear."

Val ended the call, beamed at Lily, gave her a hug. "Lily, that was just *excellent!*"

"Oh my, Val. Walker did not sound very happy."

"Oh, don't worry about him. He'll be okay. In fact, I'm starting to think we should actually bring him along. You know, just in case we need a man for something. Lord knows what, but he might be handy."

Lily was looking out the window, her eyes gray and sad.

"He'll be okay, Lily. Let me help you to the bed. You should probably nap for a while."

"He's his father's son," Lily said.

"And his father was a good man. He'll be okay, dear."

Goldie was studying her phone when Val got back to the car. "How'd it go?" she asked without looking up.

"Fine. Lily was great. I really should talk to Walker before he has a seizure, though."

Walker answered on the first ring.

"Hello, Walker. Are you okay? You sound a little stressed." Val smiled at Goldie and started her car.

"My mother just called me, Val."

"I know, Walker. I was there. Why do you think the phone was on speaker?"

"Oh."

"It's time to call Julie, Walker."

Walker was silent.

"Just tell her you want to spend some time with your mother. Sea Island is a great idea. Tell her it was yours."

"She's not going to like it, Val. She's going to flip out. I won't know what to say to her."

"Man up, Walker—it will be okay. She'll probably call me after you talk to her, and we'll figure it out. Tell her you're going to stay at the Sea Grass. I'll make a reservation for you."

"How are we going to get there? You want me to take her on a planc?"

"You're driving. Don't worry about that—I've got you covered."

"*Driving?* It's twelve hours from here, Val. I can't take my mother in a car for—"

"She's your mother, Walker. Man up."

⟞⊹ ⊹⟝

Scott Yureman was sitting at his desk with his face in his hands. When he saw Val come through the door, he uncovered his eyes and just looked at her.

"You can't be serious," he finally said.

"Of course I'm serious. I told you—I'm going on a trip."

"Where? Tahiti?"

"No, but that's not a bad idea. Maybe next year."

"You're shitting me, aren't you? You want fifty thousand bucks?"

"No, I'm not *shitting* you, Scott. I may be gone for a while."

"Yeah, I got that. But fifty K? Jesus, Val."

"Yes, Scott, I need fifty K. Last time I checked—which was this morning by the way—there was plenty of money. I don't really see why you think it's a problem."

"Are you kidding me? You don't really see why I think it's a problem? I have to sell stuff, Val. You don't have that much in the money market."

"And?"

"It's your principal, Val. It's sacred. There's no more coming in. *Nada.*"

"And?"

"And it's pretty simple—if you spend more than you earn, you're going to run out of money. I told you that last week. And my ass is going to be grass—I told you that, too."

"And I told you it will be okay, Scott. It's my money. Don't worry about it."

"And it's my job to manage your money and make responsible decisions with you. I'm sorry, Val, but I just don't find this to be the most responsible financial decision you've ever made. And that's putting it nicely."

"That's very kind of you, Scott. I really do appreciate your concern. I also abdicate you from any responsibility in this."

"*Abdicate* me? What the hell does that mean?"

Val raised her eyebrows. "*Really*, Scott? It means you're off the hook."

Yureman snorted and rubbed his eyes. "Yeah, right. Bill called me again."

"That's nice, Scott. So, if you don't mind me asking, why am I here? My friend's waiting for me. The one who really is broke. I thought my message was pretty straightforward."

"Because I wanted to see you in person and see if you really are off your rocker."

"I don't have a rocker, Scott. I think you're generalizing about old people."

"Aaah, you're killing me, Val."

"I'm sorry. You really will be okay, as will Bill and his wife and Debbie and Roger. So why am I here?"

Scott Yureman pushed a piece of paper across his desk. "Because I'm going to ask you to sign this, Val. It needs to be clear that this is your decision."

"Is this for you or for Bill?" Val asked without looking at the paper.

"It's for me," he answered, looking at his desk.

Val just looked at him.

"Ah, shit, Val. It's for both of us. Just sign it please. Pretty please."

Val took the paper and paused over the signature line. "You're not talking to Bill about my finances, are you, Scott? Because that would be a violation of my privacy."

"I wouldn't do that, Val."

"Just because you went to school together and you're friends doesn't mean you can speak with him about me. You do know that, right?"

"Sure, Val. I know that."

Val nodded, signed the paper, pushed it across the desk. "Now you're officially abdicated. And when you have a chance, you really should look up that word, Scott. You might find it handy. "

"Whatever."

"I'll stop by later this week. Thanks."

"Jesus, Val. Why can't you just go to Ocean City? It's nice there this time of year. Val? Val? Do you hear me, Val?"

Julie had called three times, Bill twice. Both had left voice messages with their last call.

Julie: "Please call me about my mother as soon as you can."

Bill: "Hi, Mom. Hope you're doing okay? Call me when you can please. I just want to touch base about a few things."

Val erased both messages and sent Goldie a text message: pick u up in five. Driving back to Starbucks, she checked her e-mail: confirmations from Eastern RV Enterprises, Nurses USA, and three Hampton Inns.

Goldie was waiting out front.

"Anything else you need to do here?" Val asked. "Pharmacy? Bank?"

"I think I'm okay for now—thanks."

"When is Rhonda getting in?"

"Around two. She's going to rent a car, so I don't need to pick her up."

"You sure? I can go with you."

"No, she's fine. She's loaded. She doesn't mind."

"Oh. Okay."

Val turned on the car speaker. "This should be interesting."

"Hi, Julie. Is everything okay? You sounded like you were upset on your voice mail."

"No, everything's not okay. I just got off the phone with my brother, and I'm about ready to throw up."

Val turned up the volume and winked at Goldie.

"I'm so sorry, Julie. What's wrong? Is there something I can help you with?"

"I hope so. Have you heard about this cockamamie idea of his? He barely knows how to get to where Mom lives and now he wants to take her away. Has he gone totally crazy?"

"I think Lily did mention something about that to me. Gosh, Julie, I thought it sounded like a nice idea. I mean, your mother's not going to be around forever."

"It might be nice if he wasn't totally irresponsible and he didn't have a drinking problem. He must be up to something. I don't know what it is, though. He can't change her will—I'm the executor of her estate, and I have her power of attorney. Plus, he's not that smart."

"Maybe he just wants to spend some time with her. She is his mother. And you know, they are pretty close."

Silence.

Goldie put her hand over her mouth and turned away.

"Julie?" Val said.

"'Close'? What in God's name are you talking about, Val? My mother's not close to anyone anymore. She can barely have a rational conversation with me for heaven's sake. And by the way, that's another thing we need to talk about. I'm really confused about her visit with Dr. Woolschlager."

"Sure, we can do that. You have all my notes, don't you?"

"Yes, but I spoke with him and—"

"I'm not so sure about Lily not being rational," Val interrupted, smiling at Goldie. "She's very lucid when she's with me, and she's still a great card player. And I've heard her on the phone with Walker. She sounds just fine."

"'The phone'? 'With Walker'?" Silence. "You can't be serious. Walker and my mother talk on the phone?"

"All the time." Val put a finger to her lips and shook her head at Goldie who still had her hand over her mouth and was straining not to laugh aloud. "Don't do it," she mouthed.

"Oh my God. This is getting weirder by the minute. I can't let him do this, Val. I'll never see her again."

"Well, I'm not sure what to tell you, Julie. He is her son."

Silence. Maybe crying, too, Val thought.

"Maybe I should go with them," Val said. "Are they going someplace nice?"

Julie was definitely crying. "I haven't even told you that yet." Sob. "He wants to take her to Sea Island. That's where my...that's where my parents got married." Sob, sob. "He thinks it's their anniversary next week." Sob, sob. "He doesn't even know when their anniversary is for heaven's sake."

"Let me talk to Lily, Julie. She'll tell me if she really wants to go. And maybe I should talk to Walker, too. Try not to worry about it."

Sob, sob.

Val lifted her hands and shrugged at Goldie.

Goldie shrugged back.

"I'll call you, Julie. It will be okay."

Val dropped off Goldie, pulled over in the main parking lot, sighed, and called her eldest son.

"Oh, hey, Mom. We were starting to worry about you. Are you okay?"

"Yes, thank you, I'm fine. I've just been a little busy with my friends and helping them with their appointments and things."

"Well, don't forget about yourself. How are *you* doing? Did you see Dr. Bernstein this week?"

"I did. He's fine."

"Funny, Mom. Your heart is okay?"

"I've got a little thing with my EKG, but you know he's a little of a worrywart. It's nothing major."

"Gosh, are you sure? When are you going to see him again?"

"This week. I'll let you know."

"I can go with you if you want. Just tell me when."

"Thanks, honey, but I should be fine. Really, it's not a big deal."

"Well, let me know. By the way, I was talking with Scott about some of my stuff, and he mentioned that you might be going on a vacation. That sounds nice. Where are you going?"

"I think I'm just going to the beach for a few days with my friend Sophie. There's a chance I might go to Sea Island for a few days, too, but I'm not sure yet."

"Sea Island? You mean Georgia?"

"Yes, you know, Georgia, the state right above Florida."

"Funny, Mom. Okay, well, don't overdo it."

"I feel fine. Great, actually."

"Your birthday is coming up. I was talking to Roger and Debbie and if you're going away we'd like to see you before then. Can you come over for dinner Friday night?"

Silence. Val was planning on leaving Saturday morning.

"Mom? Did you hear me?"

"Yes, sorry, I'm just thinking about my schedule. Sure, Friday would be good actually. I really would like to see you all before I go."

MO

Mo was waiting in the front pew. Val stood to the side in the back of the church until the last of the parishioners straggled out and then walked quietly down the aisle. Her eyes were closed, her hands folded across her lap. Val sat down next to her and put a hand on her thigh.

Mo's eyes opened and brightened. "Well, look what the cat drug in."

Val patted her thigh. "Good morning, dear. How are you feeling?"

"Oh, fair to middling." She moved uncomfortably on the wooden pew. "These pews are awful. I feel it in my back all day."

"Did the shot help at all? Maybe we should go see Dr. Sheldon again."

Mo made the sign of the cross. "Lord, no. I'll live with it."

"Well, we do need to see Dr. O'Connor today. I have strict orders from Mary Catherine. And I think we should call Dr. Sheldon's office and see if they can squeeze you in. That way I can keep you out longer, and we can go to lunch."

"My back does hurt an awful lot," Mo said with a smile.

"Oh, I know it does, dear. Come on—I'll help you up."

Val got a hand under Mo's fleshy upper arm and helped her stand. Upright, for a moment Mo stood still, her eyes closed, her breaths shallow and quick. Val steadied her until her eyes opened.

"Do you want to see Father Kelly before we leave?"

"No, thank you. We had a long talk on Sunday. He is such a nice man." Mo paused halfway up the aisle to catch her breath. "And so smart, too. He knew everything I was thinking. He even called Mary Catherine. That didn't go over very well."

"Oh, yes, I know. I heard all about it. That's why you need to see Dr. O'Connor today. You need official doctor approval. Or disapproval, depending on who you're asking."

Mo paused again in the vestibule. "Maybe she's right, Val. I probably should stay here. I would love to go, but I just don't know if I can do it."

Val helped Mo down onto a bench near the front door. "You'll be fine, dear. I have it all planned out. And it will be so much fun. We might even go to Vegas after all. I'd love to see you and Sophie at the tables."

"I just don't know, Val. Las Vegas? My word."

"Let's talk about it at lunch. Sophie needs to get out before she goes off on one of the aides again."

Cheryl, Dr. Francis O'Connor's nurse of thirty-two years, poked her head through the door to the waiting room and said Dr. O'Connor would see them in his office.

"Oh my," Mo said under her breath. "I've never been in his office."

Val helped her stand. "It is a little bit like going to see the principal. I hope Mary Catherine's not in there."

"Oh, don't even say that. I want to go to lunch."

Cheryl was waiting for them in the hall. "Is everything okay?" Mo said, moving slowly behind her.

Cheryl turned her head and looked at her curiously. "As far as I know. I think he just wants to talk with you."

Dr. O'Connor was sitting behind his desk with a cup of coffee resting on one of the few available open spots. The rest of the desk was covered with stacks of thick manila patient charts and medical journals. He stood and waved them to two chairs across from him. Sitting down, his glasses resting on the bridge of his nose, for a moment he just peered at Mo.

"So, Maureen," he finally said. "I understand you'd like to go away for a little while."

Mo looked at Val. Val nodded ever so slightly. "I'd like to try, I think. Before my back gets too bad."

Dr. O'Connor nodded, his lips seeming to toy with a little smile. "And where might you go? A little birdie told me you might go to Our Lady of Lourdes. That seems like a bit of a trip for you right now."

Val straightened in her chair and looked at Mo, who gave her a little shrug.

"Well, Doctor, to be perfectly honest I did tell Father Kelly that. And of course I'd like to go there if I could. But, like you say, it is a little far, and my friends...well, you know, they're not..."

Dr. Francis O'Connor put up a hand and then sat waiting, his eyes smiling if not his mouth. "So where might you go on this little trip of yours, Maureen?"

Mo looked to Val.

"We'll probably just go to the beach for a few days," Val said.

O'Connor nodded slowly and looked to Mo whose cheeks were turning pink. "Yes, Maureen? You look like you want to say something."

"Well, Doctor, to be honest, I don't really like the sun that much. I think I'd like to go someplace where we can play cards."

"You can play cards at the beach, can't you?"

"Well, yes, but...you know, like real cards."

"Ah."

"I'm thinking Atlantic City. Maybe even Las Vegas."

Dr. O'Connor now did break into a smile. "And your friends, they're not so religious and they're gamblers?"

"Only some of them," Val said. "I'll be with her. And I have nursing care arranged if we need it."

O'Connor nodded again, looked at his pen, rolled it in his fingers. "Mary Catherine doesn't think it's such a great idea. She's not sure you're up to it. Despite Father Kelly's blessing," he added with another little smile.

Mo looked at him sheepishly.

O'Connor smiled warmly in return. "It's okay, Maureen. You're allowed to live. She'll get over it." Turning to Val, he said, "Aren't you supposed to be taking notes?"

Val took out a pad of paper and a pen.

"Maureen's heart and lungs are fine and her back pain seems manageable. Although she seems to be in good spirits, I can tell she's getting discouraged. Getting away for a few days would probably be good for her."

Val wrote quickly and looked at him. "And a little sun wouldn't be so bad? I believe her Vitamin D level is pretty low."

"Maureen could use a little sun. As long as she doesn't get burned."

"And a glass of wine or two is okay? As long as I'm with her."

"I think Maureen is old enough to have a glass of wine or two." He stood, moved around the desk, stopped in front of Mo. Then making the sign of the cross, he said, "I, Francis O'Connor, MD, give you my blessing to go away and have a good time." He put his palm on her forehead, leaned down, kissed the top of her head. Straightening, he headed to the door. "Call me if you need me, Maureen. And see me when you get back. Have fun."

⋡⋞

"The imbeciles won't let me wait out front," Sophie said, her voice echoing through the car.

Val turned down the volume on the phone and rolled her eyes at Mo.

"You need to come in and sign me out. Christ, it's as bad as Lily."

"Lily didn't go hiking on River Road, dear. It's a little different."

"Yeah, well, it's no different to me. Out of here, Val. You said out of here."

"Next week, sweetness. Don't mess up. I'll be there in five."

Val's phone rang—Mary Catherine. "It's your mother, Mo. Do you want me to answer it?"

Mo looked at her watch. "No. Let's get Sophie and have lunch first."

Sophie was sitting in the nursing station glaring out through the large bay window. She stood as soon as she saw Val and started to walk out.

"Hold on a minute, Mrs. Horwitz," Velma said. "Mrs. Kantor still has to sign you out."

"What is this, a penitentiary? I pay a lot of money to live here."

"I don't make the rules, Mrs. Horwitz. You know that." Velma handed Val a clipboard and a pen.

"You know I'm not coming back, Velma. So what's the big deal?"

"The big deal is you'll get me fired, and of course you're coming back. We'd miss you to death."

"Don't give me any ideas."

"Oh, stop it, Mrs. Horwitz. And don't forget, Roz said you need to be back by three." Velma looked at the both of them. "And no wine. She said to make sure I told you that."

"How about four? I'll slip you a twenty."

"Three, Mrs. Horwitz. Please don't make me call Roz if you're not here."

"We'll be back," Val said, taking Sophie by the arm.

"Roz, schmoz," Sophie said as they walked out. "Out of here, Val. You said out of here."

"We're going, sweetness. We just have to break the news to Roz. We'll talk about it at lunch. I have some ideas."

Sophie opened the back door of the Lexus and slid in. "I hope you're ready to start drinking, Mo," she said. "Gotta get ready for Vegas, you know. Twenty-four seven."

"Mo was just cleared by Dr. O'Connor to go away," Val said, starting the car. "She even told him she was going to Vegas. Mo, I still can't believe you said that. I know you have a hard time fibbing, but Vegas? I thought he was going to pee in his pants."

"Way to go, Mo. If I told Andrew I was going to Vegas, he'd probably put me in the loony bin."

"Anyway," Val went on. "Mo is all set, Lily's all set, and Goldie can do whatever she wants. That just leaves you, sweetness."

"Would you please quit calling me sweetness? I could call you some names too, you know."

"Like?"

"Like big fat liar."

"I'm not fat, sweetness."

"Don't rub it in. Let's go eat. I'm starving. Is Goldie coming?"

"No. Rhonda came up from Florida. I sent her a text about lunch, but I haven't heard back from her."

"Imagine that."

"Well, if we don't see her today hopefully, we'll see her tomorrow."

"Right," Sophie said. "With her new underwear and night-gowns. I want to meet this Rhonda."

"Mo, hit him up for some Valium and some sleeping pills. He knows your back is killing you."

"She'd probably have to get another shot to do that," Val said. "You want a three-inch needle in your back?"

"I wouldn't mind. Come on, Val. Anything for the team."

"I think there's plenty of that stuff around, Sophie. I just want to get her in and out, so we can tell Mary Catherine we were there."

"I'd do it."

"Stop it, Sophie. You need to come in with us and sit in the waiting room. You can think about what you're going to say to Roz."

"Oh, I know what I'm going to say to Roz. You bet your booty I do. How about bye-bye."

"You should not have had that second glass of wine. You get a little feisty, you know. Come on, we're late."

The waiting room had one empty chair. Val put Sophie in it and went to the check-in desk and explained that Mo couldn't sit because she was in too much pain. Within a minute a nurse led them back to an exam room and gave Mo a drape.

"You didn't get any relief from the injection?" Dr. Sheldon asked as he strode into the room.

"A little maybe." Mo was in the drape and sitting in a chair.

"Where are you hurting? I thought you were having trouble sitting."

Mo looked at Val and rolled her eyes.

"She is," Val said, "but she has trouble standing for very long too."

"Can you stand for a minute? Show me where you hurt with one finger."

Mo struggled to her feet and put an index finger on her lower back.

"Same place. Well, it's a little soon, but I can give you another shot."

Mo looked to Val again.

"Do you want to wait a few more days, Mo?" Val said. "See how it feels?"

"Oh, Val, I don't know what to do."

Val looked to Dr. Sheldon. "Can you give her something to make her more comfortable for a few days?" she asked. "A muscle relaxant or something. I know she's having trouble sleeping. I don't know what you use these days, but I know Valium used to help me when I had a bad back."

"Sure, but if you're in that much pain, Mrs. Flanagan, then I really should inject it again. I think it would help."

Val looked at Mo and shook her head no. "You don't want to go through that again, honey."

Mo looked at Sheldon. "You're the doctor. You want me up on that table again?"

Dr. Sheldon picked up a phone and asked for a nurse. "Yes, please. On your side if you can."

"What are you so huffy about? You know I was kidding."

"I'm not so sure you were, and it doesn't really matter what I think. She didn't think you were, and she's the one who got the shot."

"Well, if we're going away, she might need it. Did you ever think about that? I know you've got this big trip planned, and it all sounds great, but maybe she is worried about going. She has a hard enough time here as it is."

"She doesn't have to go if she doesn't want to. She knows that. It will be good for her to get away."

"You mean it will be good for you to have her away."

"You really are in a foul mood." Val pulled into the parking lot of the Westwood Retirement Home and stopped well before the front door. "You need to use this," she said, handing Sophie a bottle of Scope spearmint mouthwash. "And be nice when you go in. Unless you want to stay here, too."

"Fat chance," Sophie said, gargling the mouthwash. She opened the car door and spit it out onto the pavement. "Are you sure you can't take me tomorrow?"

"Yes. Roz is adamant about going with you. I think it's better anyway. Let her hear everything, and then we'll talk. I suspect you'll be going to Andrew after she finds out you want to go away. Maybe I can take you to that."

Val pulled up to the front door. "Make sure you go in and say hello to Velma."

"Velma, schmelma."

"Be nice, sweetness. You can be in Vegas next week."

SOPHIE

As she did almost every night now, sometime before her room would start to gray with the first bits of dawn, Val stirred in her bed waiting, waiting, for Jules to come alive. Sometimes he was so close that she could taste him; other times so distant that she physically ached for him next to her. She hated the Jules-wasting-away dream and always tried to force herself out of it, but it was often there these nights as well, its aftertaste bitter for the rest of the day. Now, though, he was strangely absent. Some other face, some other form, was flitting around inside of her head.

And now into her space, into her kitchen, her room, her bathroom. A woman, gray and faceless, moving from room to room, opening drawers and cabinets, bending and twisting. She was in her bedroom now, right next to her, close enough to touch. Thump, thump, skip, thump, skip, thump. The woman had her purse and was opening it right in front of her. Sophie, she screamed and reached out to grab her arm. But she was gone. Val gasped, woke, her heart banging, her breaths short and quick. She fumbled on her nightstand, found the plastic bottle of nitroglycerin tablets, put one under her tongue.

Thump, skip, thump, thump, skip, thump. Slowly, calmed by the sudden inflow of blood into the aging muscle, her heart started to calm. Thump, thump, thump.

She looked for her purse—it was still there in the chair next to her bed. She closed her eyes and tried to pull the dream back together, but the rapping in her chest was suddenly back, now reverberating up her neck and into her head. She took out another nitroglycerin tablet and lay still. Thump, thump, skip, thump.

"Oh," the pharmacy assistant said when she looked at the prescriptions that Val had placed on the counter. "I thought these were for you."

"They're for my friend, Mrs. Flanagan. She's just getting out of the hospital, so I'm picking them up for her."

The young woman started typing on her computer.

"She should be in there. I brought some prescriptions over here last week for her."

The pharmacy technician hit a few more keys. "There she is. But we don't have any insurance information."

"It's okay. I'm just going to pay for them."

"Are you sure? It will only take me a minute to put it in"

"It's fine. Thank you anyway."

She hit a few more keys. "Okay, let me just double-check her date-of-birth then. Do you know it?"

"July twelfth, 1936."

She looked at the prescriptions again. "I love Dr. Sheldon. He's so nice."

"Yes, he is. He's very nice."

"Is generic okay?"

"Sure."

"It'll be about twenty minutes."

"That's fine. I'll come back later today."

Val walked out and went to Starbucks. She texted Goldie: Lunch today with Rhonda? She took out her iPad, a notebook, and went to MapQuest. She pulled up the route again to Las Vegas, Nevada, and found where she had left off in southern Virginia. She tried to space the towns no farther than fifty miles apart and close to the interstate. Then she searched for hotels in each town. It took her almost an hour to get through Tennessee. She was about to enter Arkansas when Roz called.

"Val, Val, are you there?"

Val could not tell if she was yelling or crying. She got up and walked outside.

"Roz? Are you okay? What's the matter?"

Roz was apparently in her car on speakerphone.

"I'll tell you what's the matter," came Sophie's voice, distant but clear enough. "I'm not doing it. No one's cutting my head open, let alone my brain."

"Mom, *what* is wrong with you? You heard the doctor. It might rupture."

"Good, I hope it does. Bye-bye—short and sweet."

"Oh my God—I can't take this anymore. Val, you need to talk to her. She's impossible."

"Roz, maybe you should turn off the speaker."

"She won't let me. She wants to hear everything we say."

Val smiled and shook her head. "Sophie," she said loudly, "will you please let Roz talk."

"Oh, don't please me. Since when did you get so polite?"

"*Mom!*"

"What happened, Roz? Did the neurosurgeon say she needs surgery?"

"Yes—he wants to do it next week."

"So, what's the problem?"

"I'm the problem," came Sophie's voice again. "It's *my* head."

"Sophie, you're going to have to do it," Val said. "You know that."

"You hear her, Mom?"

"Yeah, I hear her. I hear lots of things. Most of them are stupid."

"Oh my God. She's like a little kid."

"Then put me in my room and leave me alone."

"Okay, Mom. Let it rupture. Do what you want. I can't take it anymore."

"*You* can't take it anymore. How do you—"

"Roz," Val interrupted. "I have an idea."

Silence.

"I suspect Sophie just needs a break for a couple of days. She's had a lot going on. Why don't you go ahead and schedule the surgery, and I'll take her away for a few days before it. I think she'll feel better then. What do you think, Sophie?"

"I think you're both out to lunch. How many times do I have to tell you—I'm not doing it?"

"Well, then, Roz, maybe you should move her to a different place where they have more medical help."

"Oh, that's nice, Val. I wish I had more friends like you."

"Well, it's up to you. We're all trying."

Silence.

"Depends where we're going. I'm not going to some health spa."

"I really don't think that's a good idea, Val. It could rupture any day."

"Roz, not to be grim, but if it's going to rupture before the surgery, I don't think it really matters where it happens."

"Oh, that's nice," Sophie said. "You're really on a roll."

"How about the beach, Sophie?"

Silence, again.

"We'll relax and talk, and you'll feel better."

"If you're talking about Atlantic City, I'm in."

"I just don't know, Val. Val? Val? Are you there, Val?"

"I'm here. Sorry, I was just thinking. I have a suggestion, Roz. I think this is a little too emotional for you and Sophie. Why don't you see what Dr. Crawford has to say? He's very careful. If he doesn't think it's a good idea, then he'll say so."

Silence.

"Roz?"

⟞⟝ ⟞⟝

"That didn't take long," Val said when Sophie opened the door to her Westwood apartment.

"It never does with her."

"What time is your appointment?"

"Three. He's fitting me in."

"Oh, great. Bring a book."

Val's phone chimed. "Oh, look who finally found time to respond to her texts," she said, looking at the text alert that had just popped up. She tapped on the screen and put the phone closer to eyes. Goldie: Can u take me to an appt. Monday morning?

"What, she finally got hungry after all day in the hotel room?"

Val shook her head and texted her back: Sure. What time? Then to Sophie, she said, "No, she wants me to take her to an appointment on Monday."

"Let me guess, her lawyer."

"She didn't say."

Text from Goldie: 11:00 Downtown. Pick me up at 10:00?

Val: Sure. C u then. What about lunch?

Goldie: Not sure yet. Let me get back to you.

"She's not sure about lunch," Val said.

"I guess shiva's over," Sophie replied. "If it ever started."

Val nodded. "I think so. Let me just use your bathroom, and then we'll go." She set her purse down carefully on Sophie's desk and put the strap on a piece of notepaper.

"Don't mind the mess. This ain't a hotel, you know."

Val closed the door and waited for a minute as she looked around. Vanity above and below the sink; tray of medication bottles and vitamins on the sink proper. She flushed the toilet, turned both sink faucets on, opened the cabinet above the sink. Toothpaste, deodorant, cotton swabs, Q-tips, miscellaneous bits of makeup—no envelopes or medication bottles. She opened the cabinet below the sink: hair dryer, curlers, minipads, toilet paper.

She looked to the medicine tray and turned the bottles, so she could read the labels: Baby aspirin, Crestor, Lopressor, Norvasc, Amaryl, Prilosec, Vitamin D, Vitamin B complex, Centrum Silver multivitamin.

"You taking a nap in there or what?" came Sophie's voice through the door.

Val turned off the faucets and opened the door. "Relax, sweetness. I was working on my hair. I need to see Francoise before we go away."

"Well, at least you have some. I'm going to have to start using that Rogaine pretty soon."

Val picked up her purse, which had clearly been moved and turned, the strap inches away from the note paper. "Ready, dear?"

"I'm always ready, honey. Come on—let's go."

Dr. Andrew Crawford seemed perturbed that Val was sitting in the exam room with Sophie. He looked from Val to Sophie and back.

"She's my stand-by," Sophie said. "You know, so there's no funny business."

Dr. Crawford did not smile. "Where's Roz? She asked me to fit you in today."

"I don't know. Getting her hair done, getting her nails done."

No response.

"This is supposed to be an unbiased evaluation, Andrew. Roz can't be here. Val is my best friend. Val, this is Andrew. Andrew, this is Val."

Val stood and extended her hand. "It's so nice to meet you, Dr. Crawford. I've heard so many great things about you."

Crawford nodded and looked at them again.

"I'm getting senile, Andrew. You know that. If you don't mind, I'd like her to stay."

Crawford shrugged and turned to Sophie. "So, let me get this straight. You have a fairly large aneurysm in your right superior temporal artery that might rupture at any moment, and you want to go to Atlantic City. Is that about right?"

"Pretty much. I might want to go to Vegas, though. Too many memories in Atlantic City. That's where I went on my honeymoon."

Crawford nodded. "Vegas," he said.

"Las Vegas. It's in Nevada. But don't tell Roz that. This is confidential, right?"

"And do you believe you are of sound mind, Sophie? You just said you're getting senile, and we know you have a brain aneurysm. And we know you were out walking on River Road at midnight two weeks ago, and you didn't know where you were or why you were there."

"I absolutely did know why. I was going to meet Val."

Crawford raised his eyebrows. "Right. So, what I'm asking you is, why are you here? As your doctor, how could I possibly think it's safe for you to go? What do you want me to do? And don't say you want me to tell you it's okay to drink wine in Las Vegas."

"Roz made the appointment, Andrew, not me."

"Well, we are both in a little bit of a difficult situation. Are your mental faculties intact enough that you're able to make a rational decision for yourself? Or are you senile and also possibly mentally impaired by your aneurysm? Which, if the latter is the case, it means Roz and I are legally and morally bound to declare you incompetent to make such a decision. And, in fact, if the latter is truly the case, perhaps we should have you transferred to another facility or to Roz's."

Silence.

"I'm not trying to be difficult, Sophie. I just want you to see our dilemma. Which, by the way, we're in only because we care about you."

Sophie nodded. "I do appreciate all of that, Andrew. Believe me, I do." She paused, looked at her hands, looked up. "Andrew, do you know what the success rate is for fixing the aneurysm in my brain? That is, without making me a gork."

"Probably pretty good. Otherwise they wouldn't do it."

Sophie stared at him for a moment. "That would be a no, I think. Have you ever taken care of a gork? I mean, really taken care of one. Not as a doctor. I mean like changing diapers and wiping poop off their ass and picking up all their meals from the front of their shirt?"

"I get the visual, Sophie."

"Well, the neurosurgeon told me that there was *approximately* a seventy percent chance that the surgery would be completely successful. There's a ten percent chance I could die in the operating room or afterward, which is not a big deal. In fact, if that was a little higher, I might take that chance. And there's a twenty percent chance that I could—how do you all say it—end up with a neurologic deficit. That would be a gork."

"And the chance of your aneurysm rupturing and killing you is?"

"No one knows. It might, it might not."

"So you don't like the odds, is that what you're telling me?"

"Andrew, what I'm telling you is that if I'm going to die in the next few weeks, then I'd rather die at a craps table in Las Vegas with a glass of wine in my hand than in an operating room or in some home with a tube down my throat. Do you get that visual?"

Dr. Andrew Crawford nodded. "And what about when you come back?"

"Then we'll talk about it again. I promise."

"So you want me to tell Roz that it's okay for you to go away?"

"Yes, Andrew, that is what I'd like you to do. And then if you don't mind, I'd like you to write me some prescriptions. I get anxious when I travel."

GOLDIE

V al was just a few minutes away from Goldie's condo when her phone rang: 301-578-9743. She did not recognize the number, so she let it go and waited for a voice mail. A minute later her phone chimed with a new voice mail.

She parked in the front driveway of the condo complex and sent Goldie a text that she was out front. With the early September air warm, the August humidity tempered, she sat with the windows open. It was in fact a beautiful day—too nice to wait inside the car. She pulled up farther in the driveway, turned off the car, got out, walked to a bench in a small garden between the driveway and the condos.

She checked her phone—no new texts or e-mails. She looked at the front door—no Goldie. She tapped on her voice-mail screen and then on the unknown number:

"Hi, Val, this is David. I'm sorry to bother you, but I just wanted to touch base about my mother. Ever since my father died, she's been acting a little strange, and I guess we're getting worried about her. She wasn't around much for shiva, and she doesn't talk much anymore, particularly about moving in with us. We can't afford her condo, and there's almost nothing left in their estate. And she just basically disappeared for the last couple of days. She said her friend Rhonda was in town, so that's good I guess."

Goldie came out, spotted Val, headed toward her. Her hair looked newly cut and styled. She was wearing a black short sleeve shirt and what looked like new jeans and shoes. Val put up a hand and pointed to her phone. Goldie nodded and went to the car.

"…Anyway, we think she's really depressed and sort of lost without my dad around. She said she was going out with you today, so we were wondering if maybe you could call us later. Call me I guess, and let us know what you think. Thanks, we really appreciate it."

Val closed the voice mail, looked at her Lexus, cocked her head. "Hmmm," she said softly.

"Hi, dear," Goldie said when she got in the car. Goldie leaned over and gave her a hug. "I've missed you."

"You have?" Val pulled back and looked at her with a smile. "I sent you three texts about having lunch or coffee, and I never heard a word from you. I was starting to get worried."

"I'm sorry. I got so busy with Rhonda that the time just flew away."

Val looked at her a moment longer. "You look great. You got your hair cut and your nails done. And those are new jeans and shoes, aren't they?"

"Yes, but I still don't know if I look silly." She looked down at her jeans and shoes. "What do you think? Is it too much? I mean, I am eighty. Eighty-one, actually."

"You don't look eighty. And I don't think you feel eighty, whatever that feels like."

"No, I don't. I feel pretty good. Rhonda loves to shop. She's fun."

Val looked at her chest. "Is that a new necklace? I don't remember seeing that before."

Goldie fingered the diamond pendant resting on her new shirt. "No, I've had it for a while. I just don't wear it very often."

"Gosh, it's beautiful. Did Frank give it to you?"

"It was a present."

"It wasn't cheap—I know that. So where are we going? I know you said downtown, but tell me where."

"Twenty-Two Hundred K Street. Dr. Massamiano." Goldie looked at her watch. "We have a little time. Do you mind stopping at Starbucks for a few minutes. I want to show you some brochures before we go."

"Sure. I'd love some tea. And I want to hear all about Rhonda."

Goldie pulled a stack of glossy brochures out of her purse and set them on her lap.

Val could see the top one: Botox. She looked at Goldie. "I guess shiva's over," she said.

The baby blue script on the pristine double glass doors read: Washington Aesthetic Institute, Raphael Massamiano, MD, Director. The floor inside was marble, the rugs fine oriental, the waiting room chairs burnished mahogany. Fresh coffee, hot water for tea, and a crystal pitcher of ice water with lemons stood on a glass side table. Two women were sitting apart from each other in the waiting room, both middle-aged and polished, both absorbed in magazines.

Val raised her eyebrows at Goldie. "I hope you brought a checkbook," she said.

"Of course, dear."

Goldie went to the receptionist's desk; Val took a chair. Goldie was finished quickly—no insurance paperwork here. She sat next to Val and looked around. On the coffee table in front of them were several binders filled with photos and information on various cosmetic procedures. She picked one up and started flipping through it.

One of the other women was called into the back and then the other a minute later.

"Maybe I should get my boobs done," Goldie said.

Val looked at her chest. "What?"

"You know, a little lift, a little bigger. Think of all the new clothes I could wear."

"And why are you thinking of that now if you don't mind me asking? Did Rhonda have hers done?"

Goldie flipped another page. "I don't know. She probably did years ago."

"I don't think I need liposuction. Maybe a facelift. I'm sure he'll tell me that."

The door opened from the back offices, and a young woman who could have come out of one of the brochures called Goldie's name.

Goldie stood. "I'd really like my friend to come in with me. Is that okay?"

"Absolutely. The more the merrier."

The woman led them to a room with several computer monitors and cameras. "Is it okay if I call you Goldie?" she asked.

"Of course."

"My name is Lauren." She looked at Goldie's chart. "I understand you'd like to talk to Dr. Massamiano about Botox and Juvederm?" she asked. "And maybe talk about surgery?"

"Honey, if I can look like you, I'll do anything you want."

Lauren smiled sheepishly. "Thank you. I'm sure you can, you know."

Goldie and Val looked at each other and laughed. "Yeah, right," Goldie said. "How about we try for sixty or seventy."

"Well, let's see what we can do. First thing is, I want to take some photos of your face if that's okay. Doctor Massi—that's what we call him—can then show you on the computer what you might look like with different procedures."

Ten minutes later they were in the doctor's consultation room with Goldie's face already up on a computer monitor. Dr. Massamiano, fitted shirt open at the collar, white doctor's coat, Italian loafers, strode in all smiles. He cocked his head, eyed Goldie's face, cocked his head the other direction, eyed her face some more.

"Beautiful," he said. "If you don't have that, it is very hard." He shook his head in feigned disgust. "You don't know how hard I try sometimes. So, how can I help you, Goldie? You are already beautiful. What would you like? Would you like to look a little younger?"

Goldie took the hand mirror he gave her and pointed to the frown lines between her eyes and the creases around her mouth. "Well, for starts, I hate these. And I hate that and that."

The doctor nodded. "We can help you with that now with a little Botox and filler. That's a short-term fix. But if you really want to do something," he said, putting his thumbs on her cheekbones and pulling up, "it's this. You'd look wonderful."

"Facelift, huh."

"Just a little one. It's very simple, actually."

Goldie looked at Val; Val shrugged.

"Next year," she said. "I'm going away in a few days."

Forty-five minutes later, with ice packs on Goldie's cheeks, they made their way to the check-out desk.

"Today's services will be sixteen hundred dollars, Mrs. Tannenbaum," the receptionist said sweetly.

Goldie took a credit card from her wallet and put it on the counter.

Val stepped closer and looked at it. It looked new. It had Goldie's name on it.

"Did you run out of cash?" Val said when they were in the hallway. "I don't want you to run up a credit card bill."

"No, I'm okay. I'm just trying to save some of it."

Val nodded. *Really*, Goldie?

Val looked at Goldie, whose forehead and cheeks were swollen and starting to bruise. "Maybe you should wait in the car," she said. "I'll only be a few minutes."

Goldie put the ice packs back on her cheeks. "That's probably a good idea."

Val got out and went straight into Scott Yureman's office. He was on the phone, his back to her. He turned, saw her, ended his call abruptly.

"I can wait," Val said. "You know us retirees—nothing but time."

Yureman slid an envelope across his desk. "Don't spend it all at once. There's not much left."

"I'll try not to, Scott."

Val reached in her purse, took out her own envelope, slid it across his desk. "I'd like you to hold onto this for me please."

Yureman eyed the envelope suspiciously. "Are you firing me?"

"Never, Scott. Just some instructions and notes in case I'm away, and you need some things in writing."

"So…you want me to open it or not open it? I don't get it, Val. Sorry."

"Just hold onto it for now, Scott. I'll let you know."

"Does Bill know about this?"

"About what?"

He eyed the envelope again. "About whatever that is."

"No. Should he?"

"I don't know. Should he?"

"I gave it to you, Scott. Not Bill."

Yureman picked up the envelope, felt it, frowned. "Are there keys in here?'

"Maybe. Just put it in your desk, Scott. Don't worry about it." Val turned to leave.

Yureman covered his face with his hands and rubbed his eyes, over and over again. "You're killing me, Val. Jesus. You're just killing me."

⊷ ⊶

Val had already called her bank to let them know she was coming with a large check and that she wanted a lot of cash.

The branch manager was waiting for her in his office. "Are you sure this is how you'd like to handle this, Mrs. Kantor? It's a lot of cash to be carrying around. We can give you travelers checks or money orders."

"Cash is fine. I'll be okay with it. Thanks anyway." Val took out the envelope from Scott Yureman, endorsed the check, gave it to the manager. "I'd like to deposit twenty-five thousand in my checking account, and I'll take twenty-five thousand in cash."

"It was good you called ahead. We had to get more cash." The manager took the check and went into the back of the bank. When he came back, he had a money bag that he set on his desk. He opened it and counted out twelve packs of twenty crisp hundred dollar bills with a paper wrap around the center of each pack and then one smaller pack. Then he did it again. "Twenty-five thousand," he said, looking at her purse. "Do you want a bag or something?"

Val took the stacks and put them in her purse. "No, thank you. This is fine. Thank you very much. I appreciate it."

"You said on the phone you wanted to do something with your safety deposit box?"

"Yes, I came in the other day and got a new signature card." She took the card out of her purse with Scott Yureman's printed name and his forged signature and gave it to the manager. "I'm just adding another authorized name to the box. He's the co-executor of my estate."

The manager took the card and looked at it. "No problem. I'll put it with the others today."

Val picked up her purse. "Thank you for everything. I appreciate it."

"Our pleasure, Mrs. Kantor. We appreciate your business. Have a nice trip, wherever you're going."

"We will, thank you. I think it's going to be a lot of fun."

Val dropped Goldie off and then called David from the parking lot, hoping he wouldn't answer, and she could just leave a voice mail. No such luck.

"Hello, Val?"

"Hi, David. I got your message this morning. Your mom and I spent a lot of time together today. I'm not sure she's quite as depressed as you might think, but certainly she's depressed at some level. I suspect that's fairly normal at this point. She spent a lot of her life with your father."

"Most of her life, actually. That's why we're worried about her. You don't think she would do anything to…to hurt herself, do you? You know what I mean."

"No, I don't think so. There are just a lot of changes now with Frank passing and her probably having to move out of her place."

"Yes, we realize that. And we feel terrible about that, but we just can't afford it. I don't really know where she got the money for this month. We were going to stop the lease at the end of August."

"I suspect her friend Rhonda helped her, but I don't really know. Anyway, she understands the situation. We're thinking about going away for a few days, maybe to the beach. I think that would be really good for her. It will give her a chance to regroup."

"Maybe getting away from here for a few days would be good for her. She had a hard time handling shiva."

"Yes, I know she did. I'll call you when we get back. Try not to worry about her, David. She'll be okay."

VAL

Thump, thump, skip, thump, skip, thump, thump, thump!
She forced her eyes to stay shut. He was so close, sitting in his chair on the hard sand where the low waves were breaking around their ankles and rolling under their chairs onto the gentle incline of the beach. But she could not bring him closer, and, for a moment, all she could grasp were the bubbling sheets of greenish-gray water sliding over the sand as the earth, spinning on its axis, pulled them from the sea. For just the briefest of seconds, at their farthest reach for freedom, they would lie still, clinging valiantly to the sand. Until there was no more fighting the mother force. Succumbing to her relentless pull, they would slowly retreat leaving little piles of wet dark sand on the back of their heels.

Jules seemed oblivious to the coming and goings of these tendrils of the sea, his golden bald head turned to the wide expanse of the ocean stretching out to the horizon. The horizon that seemed endless in the waning light of the early evening.

Thump, skip, thump, thump!

She reached for him and his head turned toward her, enough to see the gray stubble of his beard and the curve of his nose and the sagging folds of skin in his heavy jowl. But she could not touch him, get to him. She tried to slide her chair closer, but it was immovable, mired in the wet sand, the aluminum frame digging tenaciously into the earth.

Jules! Jules!

His big bronze head stayed still, as much as she cried. Then slowly it turned back to the horizon, his gaze relentless on the softening pink edge of the sea.

And then he was gone. He had no choice. The muscle in her chest was wild, beating and thrashing about like a trapped animal. Sweating now, she reached for her nightstand, for her nitroglycerin, and put two under her tongue.

Thirty seconds passed, her breaths still hard and little beads of sweat coalescing on her forehead. A minute, two minutes, and the live thing in her chest finally started to calm.

When she could breathe again, she pulled herself upright onto her pillows. It was time to get up. The day was filled with appointments. And then she had to make her way out to Frederick, Maryland, where a two-ton Autumn Gold Winnebago Journey had her name on it.

⇥ ⇤

Dr. Harold Bernstein was playing checkers with his stethoscope again. Down, up, down, pause, hop, pause, hop, pause a little longer, hop. He took it off her breast, made a note in her chart, moved it to her flank to listen to her lungs. Hop, hop, hop. Finally he was done. He took it out of his ears, let the earpieces rest on his neck, cleaned his glasses.

"May I get dressed, Harold?"

"Yeah, sure. I'll be back in a minute. Don't go anywhere."

"Promise."

He returned to the exam room in five minutes, sat down, folded his hands in his lap, looked at her with his serious face. "It's getting worse, Val. The EKG shows it, and I can hear it. I'm sure you feel it as well. Are you sure you've been feeling okay?"

"I'm good, Harold. I'm looking forward to going away."

Dr. Bernstein cocked his head, furrowed his brow. "What?"

"I'm going away for a little while with some of my friends. Before they can't travel anymore."

"When? You need an echo and a stress test."

"Tomorrow maybe."

"'Tomorrow'?"

"Tomorrow. First thing. I'll get them done as soon as I get back. Promise."

"Val, you're going to need a pacemaker. I told you that the other day. You're having PVTs every thirty seconds. You already go into SVT from time to time. You're going to go into V-Fib. You need a pacemaker."

"You need a translator, Harold."

"Oh, you know what I mean. Your heart's going whacky. I want to get the pacemaker in next week. I've already talked to the cardiologist. That's what I was just doing."

"As soon as I get back. I promise."

Dr. Bernstein screwed up his face and shook his head. "I'm sorry, Val, I don't get it. Why don't you just wait a week or two? This is more important, frankly. I mean, I'm not trying to be dire, but your heart is trying to tell us something. It needs help."

"Then listen to it, Harold. I am. I'm going to go away with my friends for a little while before they're too sick or too senile to go away. Then I will come back and get the echo and stress test and pacemaker and whatever else I need."

Bernstein shook his head and shrugged. "Okay. It's against medical advice. I want you to know that."

"I need some prescriptions, Harold."

"Yeah, you do. You need to go up on your atenolol, and you need to go up on your Vasotec again. And I'm telling you, get a pill box or write it down or something. They're controlling your rate and your pressure. If you miss doses, they're going to go through the roof. Your heart can't take it."

"I have a pill box, Harold. It's quite convenient, actually. It has two rows—one for the morning and one for the evening. Simple."

Bernstein made a noise and took out his prescription pad.

"I need some more Xanax, Harold. You're stressing me out."

Val took a cab to the Frederick, Maryland, location of Eastern RV Enterprises. There were three Winnebagos in the parking lot. She had studied the Winnebago website enough that she recognized what was most likely her Autumn Gold Winnebago Journey. She had the cab drop her off in the lot, and she walked around it for several minutes. It looked nice. She thought it was going to be perfect.

The office was empty except for a middle-aged paunchy man wearing a black Eastern RV Enterprises T-shirt sitting behind the desk. Billy, his name tag said. He looked up, glanced at the door closing behind Val, looked back to his desk.

Val stood at the desk patiently until he looked up again. He moved his head to look behind her and then glanced at a piece of paper taped to the counter in front of him.

"Mrs. Beauchamp?"

Val shook her head no.

"Mrs. Crandall?"

No.

He looked at the counter again and then at the third set of legal-sized papers on the desk. "Valerie Kantor?"

She nodded.

He looked at the door again and looked at Val.

"You're alone?"

"I am."

He nodded slowly. "You're going to drive that 'Bago to Vegas or Florida?"

"I am."

"By yourself?"

"Yes. All by myself. Is that a problem, Billy?"

He looked at the forms again, shrugged, stood. "I guess not. You got pretty good coverage. You ever driven a 'Bago?"

"No. I've driven a bus, though."

He nodded slowly again. "Maybe we should drive it around the block a couple of times before you take off. Maybe back it up a time or two. It ain't no minivan, you know."

Val smiled. "That would probably be a good idea. And maybe you could show me how the steps work and some other little things like that."

"Sure, I can do that." Billy called into the back, and a young woman came out. "Candy, can you watch the desk for a few minutes. I'm going to show this nice lady a few things about her 'Bago."

Thirty minutes later, after four trips around the block, eight parking and backing up exercises and a complete tour of the 'Bago, Val pulled out of the lot and headed for Interstate 270. She maneuvered the 'Bago Journey onto the entry ramp, adjusted her mirrors, merged into traffic. She pushed on the accelerator and the two-ton RV slowly picked up speed. She checked her mirrors again, adjusted the high padded leather driver's seat, turned on the radio. A car pulled up beside her, and a young woman in the front seat gave her a thumbs up.

Val gave her one back and smiled. "No, they don't," she said aloud. "Not even diddly-squat."

⊷╬╀⊶

Bill opened the door and hugged his mother. Stepping back, he looked at her. "Are you sure you're not losing weight?"

164

"I don't think so. I feel fine."

"Granny, Granny." Charlotte, Debbie's youngest daughter, came running through the entry hall and hugged her grandmother. "Look," she said, pointing down the hall where a "Happy Birthday Granny" banner was hung across the entry to the kitchen. "Look what we did." Val took her hand and walked down the hall. "It's beautiful, Charlotte. Thank you so much."

Debbie came out of the kitchen and hugged her mother, followed by Roger.

"It smells wonderful," Val said. "Is Kristen cooking?"

Roger looked to Debbie. "She's reheating. It's catered."

"Oh, how nice." Val went into the kitchen and said hello to Kristen, Bill's wife, and then found the rest of the grandchildren. Soon they were all sitting around the oval dining room table.

"So, are you still going away?" Bill asked near the end of dinner.

"I am. We're leaving in the morning."

"Tomorrow morning?"

Val nodded. "Unless something happens between now and then. You never know these days."

"Wow, you're not wasting any time. Are you going to let us know where you're going, or is that a secret?"

"Of course. Sophie and Mo want to go to Atlantic City, so we'll go there for a few days. Then Goldie wants to go to the beach, so we'll probably go to Cape Lewes for a few days on the way back."

"A girls' trip," Debbie said. "How fun. I'm jealous."

"You're driving, I presume," Bill said.

"Yes. Sophie and Mo don't do too well with that anymore. Goldie's fine though if I need a break."

"Well, be careful, and let us know if you need anything." Bill looked around the table at the kids. "Your, uh, your files are all in the same place?"

Looking at her coffee cup, Val nodded. "In the closet."

"Bill," Debbie said, "this is not the time for that. Why are you so morbid anyway?"

"Morbid and responsible are two different things, Deb."

"Whatever. You can have that conversation later."

"Well, okay, but she's leaving in the morning. And I'm the one responsible for all that stuff."

"It's okay, Debbie," Val said. "That's the reality these days."

Debbie shook her head. "Where are you staying in Atlantic City, Mom?

"One of those newer places. The Bellagio, I think it is."

"Wow," Bill said. "That's nice. You all aren't messing around."

"It's not that expensive," Val said. "It's only a thousand a night."

"A thousand a night," Kristen said. "You're staying in a hotel that costs a thousand dollars a night?"

Val looked at her. "Well, yes. I thought that was pretty good. The suites are even more. We still might upgrade to one if we don't like the rooms."

"Rooms? You're not sharing a room?"

Val laughed. "Oh my gosh, no. We're too old for that. And Mo and Sophie both snore like bears, for heaven's sake."

Kristen got up and started to clear the table.

"Okay, Mom," Debbie said. "Time to open your presents."

An hour later it was time to go. Val took each grandchild onto her lap and hugged them hard. She said thank you and good-bye to Kristen, kissed Bill good-bye, hugged him a little harder than usual. She held Debbie in her arms for a good thirty seconds.

"Are you okay?" Debbie said. "Your eyes are wet. Are you crying?"

"No, I'm fine. I'll call you, dear. Roger, honey, would you please walk me to my car?"

"Uh, sure," Roger said from the hallway where he'd been patiently waiting to say his good-bye.

Val took his arm as they walked to the car. There, she hugged him, opened her purse, took out a check for ten thousand dollars, pressed it into his hand. "Put that in your pocket, Roger. It's our little secret."

Roger looked at the check and put it into his pocket. "Mom, you're—"

"Shhh. I love you, honey. You need to always remember that. Your father and I weren't always around as much for you as for Debbie. I'm sorry about that. I know he is, too."

Roger's eyes started to tear.

"Be strong, Roger. Always. I know you are. You're more like your father than you know."

"Mom, why are you doing this? You're worrying me."

"I don't mean to, honey. I just may be gone for a while. I'll miss you."

"Okay. Have fun, Mom. I'll miss you, too."

"Be strong, honey. You can do it. I know you can."

FOUR

*Dying is one of the few things that can be done
as easily as lying down.*

Woody Allen

MO

Tim answered the door. "Hi, Val. She's waiting for you. She looks like she's going to camp."

Mo was in the living room on the couch. She had her purse, a pillow, and a large carrying bag next to her. A black suitcase was on the floor in front of her.

Mary Catherine walked in from the kitchen. "You know," she said with a little smile, "this is harder than letting Tommy go to beach week. At least we had a chaperone there."

Val raised her eyebrows. "I think I qualify as a chaperone, Mary Catherine."

"I'm sorry. I didn't mean it that way, Val. I just—"

"I'll make her behave. I promise. No shacking up, right, Mo?"

"Oh my gosh, no," she said, struggling to her feet with Tim's help. "You know I don't sleep around, Val."

"Mom! I can't believe you even said that."

Mo rolled her eyes at Val.

"Oh my God. Actually, that's not really what I'm worried about, Mom. Seriously, you're not so steady on your feet. You can't be drinking wine like you do here sometimes."

"She won't be," Val said. "We already talked about that. Early to bed, early to rise."

"Do you have all your medications?"

"In my bag."

Mary Catherine hugged her. "Have fun, Mom. Be careful." To Val, "Please call me when you get there, so I know you're safe. And please e-mail me all the hotel information." She looked at her watch. "It usually only takes about three hours. You have my right e-mail address now, don't you?"

"I do. McDunn at yahoo.com. I'll e-mail you everything as soon as I know it. I have a couple of different reservations. We want to look at the rooms first."

"Are you ready, dear?" Val said to Mo. "We need to pick up Sophie. She's probably getting antsy. You know how she is."

"So, we'll you see you in a few days?"

"Probably. We might stop by Cape Lewes on the way back for a day or two. We'll see how everyone feels."

"Mom, I thought you said you were just going for a couple of days? I don't think you're up to much more."

Mo looked to Val.

"Don't worry, Mary Catherine. We'll take care of her. And if she needs to come home, then we'll come home."

Tim picked up Mo's suitcase and bag and walked them to the car. "Have fun, Mo." He turned, looked back at the house, slipped her a hundred dollar bill. "I hear you're pretty good on the tables. I get half, you get half."

Roz opened Sophie's door. She did not look good. She looked like she'd been crying, and she was opening and closing her hands.

"You stop at I Hop or what?" came Sophie's voice from behind her. "Geez, Louise, I think I had another birthday in here."

Roz shook her head and rolled her eyes at Val. "I don't know how you do it," she said.

"Good morning, sweetness. Are you ready to go? Mo's in the car."

Sophie was sitting on her bed with a pillow and her purse and a soft carry-on bag next to her. A suitcase stood by the door.

Roz walked to Sophie's desk and picked up a folder. "All of her medical information is in here," she said. "Her medications, doctors' names, and all of their phone numbers. I also went online and made a list of hospitals and neurosurgeons between here and Atlantic City."

"That's great, Roz. I didn't think about that. Thank you so much."

Sophie looked at Val, opened her mouth, put a finger on her tongue, and pretended to gag.

"So you really don't know where you're staying yet?" Roz asked.

"I have several reservations. We want to see the rooms first. You know how picky us old people are."

"My sugar's low, Val. I need to eat."

"Mom, your sugar's fine for heaven's sake. You need to watch what you eat if anything. Val, there's also a diabetic nutrition plan in there. Her sugars are high. Dr. Crawford said he might have to put her on insulin."

"Okay, I'll watch what she eats. No doughnuts, sweetness."

Roz's back was still to Sophie. Sophie put her hand up with her thumb out, pointed it toward the door, and moved it back and forth.

"Up and at 'em, dear."

Sophie stood and Roz turned to hug her. Roz was crying again. "Have fun, Mom," she said. "Call me when you get there please."

Val looked to Sophie. It was hard to tell with Sophie's head buried in Roz's shoulder, but she thought Sophie was crying as well. "Are you ready, sweetness?" Val asked when they finally separated.

Sophie nodded and wiped her eyes. "How many times do I have to tell you? Quit calling me sweetness. You're no bowl of sugar yourself, you know."

Val picked up her suitcase. "We'll call you, Roz. Don't worry. She'll be fine."

⌐≼⊹ ⊹≽⌐

Val put Sophie's suitcase in the trunk, studied what space was left, shook her head. In the car, she said, "I think I'm going to have to drop you girls off at my place and then go get Goldie. I don't think there's enough room in the trunk. Goldie said she had a few bags."

"What, for all her new underwear? They should take up less space from what I hear."

"I think she bought some new clothes when Rhonda was here."

"Yeah, has anyone ever seen this Rhonda?"

"What do you mean, Sophie?" Mo said from the front seat. "I think I saw a picture of her once."

"Well, I'd like to see a picture of her. Yes, I would."

"I'm sure she has some photos, Sophie. Enough. If I give you a key, do you think you can help Mo into my house?"

"Sure. You got any wine open?"

"It's ten o'clock, Sophie. No wine."

"How about a bloody then? What do you think, Mo? We're on vacation."

"No bloodies either. Geez, you are like a little kid. We'll get on the road soon."

Val turned on her car speaker and tapped on her phone. "Hi, Walker. Are you at your mother's?

"Yes, ma'am," came Walker's voice after a moment.

"Is she packed and ready to go?"

"Uh, yes, ma'am."

"Okay. What's the matter?"

Silence.

"Is Julie there?"

"Yes, ma'am."

"Oh. Do you want me to speak with her?"

"Uh, yes, ma'am. That would probably be a good idea."

"Okay. Give her the phone."

"Val, I'm sorry, I'm just having a really hard time with this. I mean, Sea Island is twelve hours from here. And, I'm sorry, but—Walker, I really don't mean this in a bad way, but I have to say it—my brother just doesn't spend that much time with her."

"Well, maybe this is a good thing then. Your mother's not going to be around forever, Julie. You've been a wonderful daughter, and you've gotten to spend a lot of time with her. This may be good for your brother."

Silence.

"I'll take care of her, Julie. We'll be fine."

"Oh my God. Please call me when you get there."

"I will. Will you give me back to Walker, please? "

"Walker, go ahead and leave. Drive to my place and just wait in the parking lot for me. I wrote the directions out for you. You have them, right?"

"Yes, ma'am."

Val hung up and sighed. "I don't know about Walker. He's going to have to man up."

"Is that simpleton really going with us?" Sophie asked.

"He is. It'll be fine. I'll get him his own room wherever we go."

"No shit, Sherlock. I don't think any of us are sleeping with him. Well, I guess I won't speak for Vicky."

Val pulled up to the front door of her townhome, let Mo and Sophie out, then drove into the parking lot and pulled up next to the Winnebago. She unlocked the luggage compartment, put their suitcases in, and headed for Goldie's.

Goldie was waiting out front next to two large suitcases and two garment bags. Val popped her trunk and Goldie rolled one suitcase over to the car and then the other. They both lifted them into the trunk and put her garment bags on top.

"Someone came prepared," Val said.

"I couldn't stop packing," Goldie said. "Las Vegas, Sea Island, Florida. Casual, formal maybe. What's a girl to do?"

Val laughed. "Now that's a good question, isn't it, Goldie? Hmm. 'What's a girl to do?'"

Back at the 'Bago, Val pulled up to the side again, stowed Goldie's belongings with her help, and unlocked the RV. She parked the Lexus in her reserved spot, double-checked the windows, locked the car.

She quickly showed Goldie around the 'Bago and then went to get Mo and Sophie.

They were playing blackjack at the kitchen table with glasses of water in front of them. Val went into her bedroom to get her suitcase. She had left all of her medications out on her bathroom sink as well as the plastic bags of pills she had labeled before. She looked at them—each one of them had been moved. She thought about counting the pills, but she knew it wasn't necessary. All of the bags looked as if they had been opened. All of them would be lighter. She packed the medications in a separate black cloth zippered bag, turned off the lights, rolled out her suitcase.

"Are you girls ready?"

"Hit me," Sophie said.

Mo flipped over a card and smiled. "You owe me a dollar."

Val turned off all of her lights, locked the door.

"Oh, my heaven," Mo said when they got to the 'Bago. "Oh, my heaven."

"Sweet," Sophie said. "Now this is a ride."

Walker pulled up and put down his window. He looked from Val to the 'Bago and back. "We're going in that?" he asked.

"Yep. What'd you think we were going in, Walker? My Lexus?"

Walker looked at Mo and Sophie and Goldie, who had just appeared in the side door. "Everyone?"

"Yep."

"I thought it was just you and me and my Mom."

"Nope."

"Val, I can't—"

"Park your car over in that guest space, Walker. All the bags go in there." Val nodded to the side luggage compartment with her head.

"Val."

"Yes, Walker?"

Walker, his face flushed and sweating, looked from Val to the others again.

"Over there, Walker," Val said. "Go on. You can do it."

Val pulled the forty-one foot, two-ton Autumn Gold Winnebago Journey onto Connecticut Avenue and headed for the Capital Beltway. "Last chance," she called into the back. "Atlantic City or Vegas?"

"Vegas," Sophie said. "Hit me."

"Vegas," Mo said.

Val turned and looked around. Goldie, typing on her phone, apparently had not heard her. Lily was resting on the couch with her head back and her eyes closed.

"Walker?"

Walker was sitting up front with Val. "I thought we were going to Sea Island."

"We are. But we're going to Vegas first."

"Vegas? Holy hell, Val. I can't take off that much time from work. I'm going to get fired."

"We'll figure that out, Walker. Don't you worry about it."

At half past noon, two miles from Harrisonburg, Virginia on Interstate 81, Sophie announced that she was hungry and that it was also now afternoon and therefore socially acceptable to start drinking.

"Happy hour starts at five, sweetness."

"Five? I could be dead by five."

"We'll take our chances. McDonald's or Wendy's?"

"Micky D's. Christ, you're worse than Velma. You might even be worse than Roz."

At 6:00 p.m., after two stops for snacks and mixers, and a hundred miles short of where Val had hoped to stop for the night, Val exited I-81 at Roanoke. Lily was getting restless, as was Walker. This was probably the longest he'd gone in a long time without a drink, she suspected. Mo, after two glasses of wine, was in the back bedroom on the Queen bed snoring, with Sophie beside her. Goldie was quiet, looking out the window.

Val asked Goldie to wake up everyone and called the Roanoke Hampton Inn to confirm the reservation for four rooms that she had made. Suspecting that she might be ambitious with her driving plans, she had reservations there and at a Holiday Inn in Kingsport, Tennessee, for the first night. Goldie and Sophie flipped for the lone single room before she went in. Sophie lost.

"Oh, come on, Vicky. We're in Sticksville for Christ's sake. What do you need a single for here?"

"Fair's fair."

"Yeah, well, all I know is my luck better change before we get to Vegas."

"Come on, girls. You too, Walker. Let's get cleaned up, and we can go to that Outback right across the street. We need to be on the road early tomorrow."

Walker was looking up and down the road at the strip shopping centers on either side.

"Relax, Walker. And don't look so sad. I brought you some vodka."

Walker looked at her and smiled for the first time that day. "Really?"

"Yes, Walker, really. I'm not that mean."

⊷⊹ ⊹⊶

The morning did not start off so well. Mo had had a rough night between her back, a strange bed, and Sophie's snoring. Sophie insisted that Mo had kept her up all night with her tossing and turning and was in a foul mood. Lily, out of her environment, seemed agitated, and Val felt like she couldn't let her out of her sight. Walker, smelling like a distillery, had slept through his alarm and had to be awakened by Val shaking him hard enough to make him dizzy. Only Goldie looked fresh and cheerful.

Breakfast at The Pancake House seemed to make the morning better. Sophie, between bites of her Belgium waffle and bacon, lightened up. As Mo worked on her bacon and cheese omelet, they settled their bets from the day before and started talking about the day's games. Goldie stayed off her phone for the entire meal. Walker, after a shower and with a fresh golf shirt on, actually looked presentable and sat amiably next to his mother. Lily, with a clean white blouse and her silver hair pulled back with a new gold clip that Val had bought her, looked wonderful.

They were on the road shortly after nine o'clock. Lily and Walker joined Sophie and Mo at the table for Texas Hold 'Em. Goldie sat up front with Val. Up high in her leather seat, Val checked the dashboard as if it were the control panel on an airplane. Then she looked at her phone for the first time that morning: six missed calls, four voice mails, multiple text messages, multiple e-mails. She handed the phone and a cord earpiece to Goldie and started the 'Bago.

"Geez, I don't even know where you should start," she said. "You should probably listen to the voice mails first."

Goldie had a pad of paper on her lap and a pen in hand. She put the earpiece in, tapped on the phone, started to write. A few minutes later she took it out, looked at Val, raised her eyebrows. "I think you have a little damage control to take care of."

"Oh, I'm sure. Let's just do it all at once. Go ahead and check the texts and the e-mails."

Goldie tapped again, took a few notes, looked up.

"Julie, Roz, and Mary Catherine?" Val said.

Goldie nodded. "And Bill."

"Who's the worst?"

"I would say they're all a little upset and worried. I'd probably start with Roz. She was crying."

"Do I need to call all of them, or can we do any of it by text or e-mail?"

Goldie thought for a moment. "I would say that if you don't want a police escort pretty soon that you might want to call them."

Val sighed, took the phone, put the earpieces in her ear. "Jesus, you'd think we did something wrong," she said.

Right around 11:00 a.m., Val crossed the Tennessee line and honked her horn. "Tennessee," she announced loudly to the back.

"Holy Moly," Sophie said. "I've never been in Tennessee. Have you ever been in Tennessee, Mo?"

Mo was studying her cards. "I'll stay. What did you say, Sophie?"

"Oh, never mind. Where are we going to have lunch, Val?"

"You're not really hungry, are you? You had two breakfasts."

"This is supposed to be living time, Val. Remember? Living time. I told you I wasn't going to any health spa."

Val looked to Goldie, who had Val's iPad on her lap. "What do you think, Goldie?"

Goldie looked at the Google Earth map she'd been studying. "I think lunch in Knoxville and dinner in Nashville."

"I heard that. Knoxville? Where the hell is Knoxville?"

"An hour or so from here," Goldie said.

"An hour? I might be dead in an hour."

"I'll stop as soon as I see something," Val said. "God, you're a pain."

"Why don't you just check your phone or that pad thing?" Sophie said. "Or better yet, ask that girl in the phone. What's her name? Siri something? She'll tell you what restaurants are close by."

Val looked to Goldie. Goldie shrugged and asked Siri for the nearest restaurant to mile marker 57 on I-81. "Cracker Barrel," she said. "Ten miles."

"Praise the Lord," Sophie said with a giggle and a look to Mo. "You hear that Mo—we're in Tennessee—praise the Lord!"

"Hallelujah," Walker said sheepishly, looking at his cards.

"Amen," Mo declared.

"Mo," Val said. "My word, I can't believe my ears."

Mo made the sign of the cross and smiled. "Bless me Lord for I have sinned."

⚞ ⚟

Sophie woke up at 4:45 p.m., forty miles outside of Nashville, Tennessee. Mo, Lily, and Walker were still asleep. Val could hear her get up, use the bathroom, make her way out to the sitting area. She heard the refrigerator open, a rubbing sound, a cork popping.

"Christ," she said softly to Goldie. "What are you doing, Sophie? It's not five yet."

"We're still in Tennessee, right? We're in a different time zone. It's five at home. Hallelujah."

"You want a glass of wine, Goldie? It's the Cakebread. A hundred bucks a bottle."

"Go ahead," Val said. "I'm going to stop soon."

"Sure," Goldie said. "We are on vacation."

Val's phone rang again. She let it go. New voice mail—Julie. It went in the queue with the other three she had gotten in the last hour.

Sophie brought Goldie her glass, and they toasted Val, the others, and the fact that they were in the Central Time Zone, and it was indeed now actually 5:50 p.m. at home and thus perfectly acceptable to start drinking.

A few minutes later, there was noise from the bedroom and then the sound of the bathroom door opening and closing.

"Oh, good, Mo's up," Sophie said.

"Great," Val said softly to Goldie. "Here we go again."

A few more minutes and the toilet flushed, the door opened.

"Bar's open, Mo. What's your pleasure?"

Val rolled her eyes at Goldie.

"You want to try this Cakebread Chardonnay? It's pretty good. It's a hundred bucks a bottle."

"Oh my. Decisions, decisions."

"Did you sleep, Mo?" Val said over her shoulder.

"Yes, thank you. I feel better." Mo sat down on the couch and rubbed her eyes. "You know, Sophie, I think I'm going to have a bloody. I've been thinking about it all afternoon."

"Are you sure, Mo?" Val asked. "You just woke up."

"Breakfast of champions, right, Mo?" Sophie said, giving her a high five. "You stay right there. I'll make it. That does sound good. Maybe I'll have one after this wine."

"It's early, Sophie. Take it easy."

Lily, who'd been napping on the couch, stirred and opened her eyes. Walker, hearing the refrigerator open and close, woke as well. Walker also thought a bloody sounded great. Sophie made two and got Lily some iced tea, and they resumed their poker game.

Val's phone rang. She let it go to voice mail, but this time she handed it back to Goldie and had her take off the messages. The morning's damage control—Val's convoluted stories of having to change hotels twice—had calmed things for a while, but Julie, Roz, Mary Catherine, and Bill now all wanted definitive hotel information. Val and Goldie discussed the conundrum again—pretend they were in Atlantic City or just tell them they had changed their minds and were now going to Vegas?

Stall a little longer, they decided. Get to Vegas, or as close as they could, before they broke the news. Val dictated nebulous text messages to Goldie for all of them and put her phone away. She looked over her shoulder to the couch and table—the card game was getting animated, and, by her calculation, Mo and Walker were now on their second bloody marys, and Sophie had changed over as well.

"I think we need to stop," she said to Goldie, who was on her second glass of wine. "They're going to be looped if we don't get some dinner."

"You have a reservation in Nashville, right?" Goldie asked.

"Oh, my word, I need to use the ladies room again," came Mo's voice from the back.

"Goldie, will you please help her. I don't think we can make it to Nashville. I'm going to stop at this Holiday Inn up here."

Val eased the 'Bago over into the exit lane and up onto the access road where the Holiday Inn was visible a quarter mile ahead. There was an Applebee's next to it and a Perkins across the street. They would have to do.

She parked and walked back into the living area where Walker was now mixing drinks with instructions from Sophie.

"That's enough, Walker," Val said into his ear as she passed by. "And you need to slow down, sweetness. It's only six-thirty."

"I need to eat is what I need to do, sweetness yourself."

Goldie was still in the bathroom with Mo. Val went back out, shook her head, opened the door, put the mechanized steps down. There were plenty of vacancies at the Lebanon Holiday Inn. She got four rooms in a row on the first floor and headed back out. Walker and Sophie were already out of the 'Bago, plastic cups in their hands. Goldie was standing in the door holding onto Mo with Lily behind her.

"You're right, Mo," Sophie said. "This is a great bloody mix. We'll get some more tomorrow."

Mo let go of Goldie's arm and took a step down.

"Hold on, Mo," Val said, "Let me help you."

Mo, her right foot halfway down to the next step, looked up and paused. Val and Walker moved toward the steps, but Mo was already moving sideways, then back to gain her balance. She tried to put her foot down, but it slid on the front of the step and in an instant she was falling, her center of gravity and weight pulling her forward. She grasped at the side of the door and missed, and then with Walker and Val still moving toward her, she fell the last two feet to the pavement, her hip and side hitting the asphalt with a sickening thud, then her face with a sharper slapping sound.

For the briefest of moments, there was complete silence.

"Oh my God," Val said, reaching her first. She kneeled next to her and put her face down to Mo's. Blood was starting to seep out the corner of her mouth. "Get me some tissue or a towel," she yelled. "Come on, Walker, move."

"Oh, Mo," she said. "I'm so sorry. I'm so sorry."

Tears were leaking out of Mo's eyes. Walker returned with a towel, and Val wiped her mouth and eyes. "Do you hurt, Mo? Tell me where you hurt."

"My leg," she managed. "My hip I think."

"Can you move your leg?"

Mo moved her head an inch side to side.

A man with luggage came over. "Do you need help? Do you want me to call an ambulance?"

Val looked up, looked around, looked at Mo. "Yes, please. Call nine one one. She may have broken her hip."

Several more people arrived and then the receptionist. Val kept the towel pressed to Mo's mouth and stroked her cheek. A siren soon sounded, then another.

"Walker, take your mother to one of the rooms and stay with her. The room cards are in my purse."

An ambulance pulled in and stopped abruptly next to them. Two paramedics moved Val out of the way and leaned over Mo. A minute later one of them stood and got on his radio.

"She needs to go by air," he said. "She probably broke her leg or her hip, and she's a little out of it. I'm worried about her neck, too." He looked at his watch. "Okay. We'll stabilize her."

"By air?" Val said. "You're bringing in a helicopter?"

"Ma'am, we're forty minutes from the medical center in that ambulance. We've done this once or twice before."

Val took a deep breath. "Of course. I know you have. Whatever you think is best. Can I go with her?"

"Does she have a husband here?"

"No."

"Any family?"

"No."

The paramedic shook his head and leaned down. "I guess. Someone has to go."

⇒⊹ ⊹⇐

Val called Mary Catherine at 1:00 a.m. She took a deep breath and let her vent about the unanswered calls, voice mails, and texts without saying anything.

"Yes, there is something wrong," Val finally said. "I'm sorry." She took another deep breath, paused, rubbed her eyes. "Mo fell, Mary Catherine. She fractured her femur and her hip. She's going to need surgery. No, you can't come right away…because we're not in Atlantic City." Deep breath. "We're in Tennessee." Phone away from her ear and then back. "Because we wanted to go to the Grand Ole Opry. But that doesn't really matter right now…yes, I realize all that, Mary Catherine, and we can talk about it later. Right now we have to take care of Mo." Deep breath, pause. "All of the doctors here think it would be best if she had the surgery at home. I've already talked to Dr. Sheldon. He's ready to see her as soon as she gets there…I've taken care of all that, Mary Catherine. They think she's stable now. I've arranged for a medical air lift. It's going to leave here at six, and it will be at Reagan National at seven forty-five. There will be an ambulance there that will take her to Georgetown. That's where Dr. Sheldon wants to do the surgery." Phone away from her ear again. Pause, deep breath. "I'm sorry, Mary Catherine. It was an accident...I know that, Mary Catherine. I'm sorry...yes, I'd be there by at least seven-thirty...one more thing, Mary Catherine, just so you know. Her dentist is also going to see her at the hospital. She fractured a couple of teeth...yes, it was a bad fall. It was terrible. I'm sorry."

Val got out of the cab at the front door of the Lebanon Holiday Inn at 2:30 a.m. Goldie and Sophie were lying on their beds dozing, both still in their clothes. Val shook them gently and sat down on the edge of Goldie's bed. Goldie's makeup was smeared from tears and tissues, and she was still visibly shaken.

"Oh, Val. I knew I shouldn't have let go of her. I feel so horrible. If only I had—"

Val put a finger on her lips. "Shh. It's not your fault. It's mine. I shouldn't have let—"

"Go ahead and say it," Sophie interrupted, wiping her eyes. "You shouldn't have let me drink, and I shouldn't have made the bloodies."

Val reached over and put a hand on Sophie's arm. "You stop it, too. You were having fun. Mo was having fun." She wiped her own eyes. "It's nobody's fault. It was just a bad idea from start to finish."

"How is she?" Goldie asked, crying again.

"She's going to be okay. She broke her femur and her hip, but the orthopedist said that it's not too difficult to fix both of them. She's flying home early this morning, so she can have the surgery at Georgetown."

"What about her face?" Sophie asked. "She was bleeding out her mouth."

"She cut her tongue and broke a couple of teeth. They're going to fix all that, too."

"Oh, I feel so horrible," Goldie said, reaching for a tissue.

"We all do, Goldie. But she's going to be okay."

"So I guess you had to call Mary Catherine," Sophie said.

"I did."

"How'd that go?"

"As expected."

Val stood up, walked to the window, looked out through the crack in the drapes. "I'd like to leave if you don't mind."

"Leave? You mean now?" Goldie asked.

Val nodded. "Mo's blood alcohol was pretty high. I don't know exactly what they plan to do about it, but it sounded like someone was going to come out here to figure out what was going on. They weren't too pleased with the situation, shall we say."

"Oh. I see."

"And I really want to get Lily to Sea Island before we have to go home. Do you mind? I'd feel better."

"We're awake," Sophie said. "Let's go. What about Lily and the simpleton?"

"I need to talk to them. Can you meet me at the 'Bago?"

Goldie was already up and getting her things together. "Five minutes," she said.

Walker was in his mother's room watching TV. Lily was asleep in the other bed.

"Walker, have you had anything else to drink?"

"No, ma'am."

"Do you think you can drive that thing?"

"Uh, I guess so."

"You're sober, or pretty close?"

"Yes, ma'am. I promise."

"We need to leave, and I need to sleep for a little while. Get on Interstate 40 and go east."

"East?"

"Yes, Walker, east. As far as you can go."

"Uh, okay. You want me to just keep going."

"Yes, Walker, just keep going. All the way. Your mother wants to see the ocean."

LILY

Val was holding onto Lily's arm as they came down the front steps of the Sea Grass hotel. Sophie and Goldie were waiting for them at the bottom. Lily had traded her white silk blouse for a pink sundress and a strand of pearls and matching earrings. Her silver hair, radiant as she moved into the sunlight, was pulled back neatly in a small bun with her new gold clip.

"Okay, Miss Georgia Peach, so where's this famous porch of yours?"

"You look beautiful, Lily," Goldie said. "I don't think I've ever seen you with makeup."

At the bottom of the steps, Val faced Lily, took hold of her other arm, and looked at her for a long moment. "She is just gorgeous, isn't she?"

"That's why she's Miss Georgia Peach. You do look great, Lily. Come on, I'm hungry. Let's go see this porch, so we can eat."

"There's no rush, Sophie. We've come a long way for this. Do you want a snack?"

"No, I don't want a snack. I want some biscuits and shrimp and grits and a glass of pinot grigio. I already looked at the menu in the room. It looks great."

"Well, hold your horses. We'll eat soon enough."

"Remember I got diabetes, Val. Too bad Mo's not here. I'd take that shuttle with her. It's hot as Hades out here." She looked around at the magnolia trees and the denser brush and cypress trees flanking the property. "I bet there are snakes here, too."

"It's beautiful out, Sophie," Val said. "The walk will be good for us."

"Have you heard anything else about Mo?" Goldie asked.

"Not yet. I'm sure she'll be in the recovery room for a while. I'll call Mary Catherine if I don't hear from her soon."

They were quiet for a moment, the sun bright and hot as it rose over the magnolia trees.

"What about the simpleton?" Sophie finally asked. "Is he coming?"

"No, this is girls' time. I've got him doing some things."

"That's too bad. I guess I'm drinking alone then."

"Oh no you're not," Goldie said. "Mo's going to be okay, and we're still on vacation. I'll have a glass of wine for me and Mo."

"Haven't you girls learned your lesson yet? It's only noon."

Sophie reached over and gave Goldie a high five. "That's right, Vicky. That's what Mo would want. You know she would."

Val shook her head and took hold of Lily's arm again. "I believe we're headed toward the ocean, dear. Isn't that right?"

Lily started walking toward a brick path flanked by a row of flowering magnolia trees. "It's this way, Val."

Val raised her eyebrows to the others and then with a shrug kept up with Lily. Around the side of the main hotel, the walkway split. Neither path headed straight toward the ocean, which they could see now, but the right fork seemed more direct, and Lily was moving that way.

"Hey, Georgia, slow down, will you? Geez, I didn't know it was a race."

Lily didn't seem to hear Sophie. Holding onto Val's hand now, she was looking straight ahead.

The path wound gracefully to the right toward a large stand of cypress trees. As they came closer to the trees, the ocean was barely visible, but they could still hear the waves on the beach.

"Holy Moly," Sophie said as they reached the cypress trees. She stopped and pointed to a sign tucked off the walkway in the shadows. "You sure this is the right way, Lily?"

Val stopped Lily and looked at the sign: Alligator Environmental Area.

Lily looked around and looked toward the ocean. "Yes, honey. It's right down by the ocean."

"I didn't know they had alligators in the ocean," Sophie said. "I'm glad you told me. I won't go skinny dipping tonight. I guess everything's different down here."

"I think there's a canal back there, Sophie," Val said. "There aren't any alligators in the ocean."

They walked a little farther until Val stopped them where a narrow dirt trail veered off the walkway. At the juncture there was a wooden sign with an arrow: Swamp Viewing Deck. She looked for a moment at the brick path heading deeper into the trees, then the dirt path heading sideways toward the swamp. Turning back toward the hotel, she said, "I think we should try the other way, Lily. We might want to ask someone, too." She took Lily's arm and turned them around. "It's okay, honey. We'll find it."

Back at the split of the path near the hotel, Val stopped and called the front desk. "I see," she said after a minute. "Okay, I got it."

"You're right, Lily, that's the way you used to go to the porch. They renovated the ocean pavilion about ten years ago, and it's on the other side of it now. But he said it still looks out over the ocean."

Lily blinked several times. "I'm so sorry, Val," she said, fidgeting with her hands. "I didn't know."

"How could you, dear?" Val took her arm again, and they headed down the left fork. Lily was quiet as they walked. When they reached the ocean pavilion, they walked around to the side and found the long wooden porch studded with wicker chairs and love seats. Between the porch and the beach was a patch of grass dotted with white Adirondack chairs.

Lily stopped for a moment to look at the porch and then let go of Val's arm and crossed the thirty yards of grass to the edge of the shallow sand dune and a path heading to the ocean.

"Hey, Georgia," Sophie called after her. "Where are you going? The porch is up here. And the restaurant."

Val motioned for Goldie and Sophie to wait on the porch and caught up with Lily. "Did you see the porch, honey?"

Lily bent over and took off her beige slip-ons.

"Where are you going, dear?"

"I want to feel the ocean," Lily said. "Come with me. The sand is hard. We used to ride bicycles on it."

"I'd love to feel the ocean, Lily. It's my favorite thing."

They headed out the path through the dune and then across the fifty yards or so of sand. The sand was white and firm and gritty, then darker and harder where the shallow waves curled over it.

Holding onto Lily tightly now, Val moved them into the water until it lapped at their ankles. The lappings of the seawater were warm, comforting. They stood there, silently, the edges of the waves brushing past them as they rolled onto the beach, then out again, past them again, out again.

"Are you okay, Lily? I'm sorry the porch isn't the way you remembered it."

Lily didn't answer. She was looking out past the waves to somewhere on the horizon.

"The ocean's the same, though," Val said. "No matter what else changes, it never does."

"Where's Walker?" Lily asked.

"He's in the room, honey. Do you want him to come down?"

"No," Lily said after a moment, turning toward the beach and the porch. "I'll see him later. Thank you, Val. Thank you for bringing me here."

"Thank you, Lily. It's just lovely. I can see why you wanted to come."

Val took Lily's hand, and they moved carefully out of the water, Lily holding her dress up over her knees with her other hand.

"I wonder if they still have shrimp and grits," she said. "We used to so love their shrimp and grits."

Lily's eyes opened at midnight, as they always did. When it was in her room eight hundred miles away to the north, she would lie still, paralyzed by the sudden primordial fear of the utter unknown. It would fill her completely until the glow of the nightlight, or the small red blinking nurse's light beside her bed would flicker with some momentary element of familiarity and penetrate the void. She would slowly calm then, slowly drift back into a fragmented sleep that would end in the early dawn with the first slips of light through her eastern shades.

In Sea Island, Georgia, though, eight hundred miles away from the vague familiarities of her Tower Oaks apartment, there were no flickering nightlights. There were no little flashes of red to stem the midnight fear. Across the room, a sliver of soft light slid through the closed blinds and drapes. To her side, a faint light came from the bathroom where Val had left on a vanity light. But she did not remember that, did not know that. She moved her head but saw only strange shapes in the room slowly taking form as her eyes adjusted to the dark and the fear heightened. Deep, lost, terrifying fear. Until the delicate scents of the pillows and sheets came to her, and in an instant, she knew this place, this room, this bed, this dark. She knew she was not alone. Her parents were down the hall. She felt the crisp linens against her neck and arms and legs. Or Walker was here. Her Walker.

Her gaze moved to the ceiling where she could now make out the crystal chandelier hanging over the center of the bed. It was still now, the dangling bits of glass hanging like icicles in concentric circles from the gold frame, threatening to fall and pierce her like...like before. Like when they came alive. She closed her eyes, trying to push this upside-down chandelier out of her ravaged memory before it came alive again. But it was slowly starting to move. Gently at first, barely swaying from side to side. Then faster and faster as Walker bore down on her, pushing and pushing his hardness inside of her, this hardness that she had only imagined before, ramming it into her and slamming the bed into the headboard sending shudders through the wall and into the very insides of the crystal, jerking them in rhythm with the totally unfamiliar noises coming from deep inside of him. The guttural moans, the animal-like grunts frightening her with their intensity and purpose, and her, not knowing what else to do, grasping his shoulders, her legs apart, until he pushed so hard inside of her that some even deeper part of him exploded and she could feel the sudden gush of sticky wetness in her groin and on her thighs. And then the fear, the fear of the unknown, of the uninitiated. The fear that she was bleeding, that he had ripped her apart in this new act of theirs, of his, and that the wetness running between her buttocks was blood.

Then almost as suddenly as it had started, he was off her and on his side, his breaths heavy and fast as if he had just run to meet her on the porch. And her, staring at the now still chandelier, the burning and wetness between her legs ebbing, leaving only this strange feeling of emptiness, of some part of her having just been trampled, stolen. This feeling she was supposed to have somehow known about, to somehow have known how to manage. And as he lay there panting, this new husband of hers, the only comfort in the room was the crispness of the linen sheets on her back and buttocks and the delicate fragrance of the pillows.

The scent of the pillows. It came to her again, and she turned her head, resting her cheek on the linen. She reached out to touch him, to tell him something, even though she did not know what to say. He turned on his back, his breaths slowly calming. She could see him, wanted to touch him, but he was not there.

She looked up—the points of crystal above her were clearer now, lining up right over her, threatening to fall on her and pierce her yet again, and the fear returned. Until she saw the reflection of the little red lights in the mirror across from the bed, the little red lights shining in the dark that she had not seen before, and she calmed.

For a moment. These little arcs of neon red were different than the nurse's light eight hundred miles to the north. She looked again—though they were backward in the mirror she could recognize them as numbers. She looked at the clock on her nightstand—12:05, it said. She ran her arm up and down the sheets. He was gone. Or…or he'd never been there. He was waiting for her on the porch! He was waiting on the shadowed steps of the porch as he always did. She looked at the clock again—12:06. She was late.

She sat up and moved to the side of the bed. She stood, oblivious for the moment to Val under the covers in the bed beside her. She parted the heavy drape covering the window and then parted a single blind. The moon, full and bright, illuminated the manicured lawn and walkways below like a floodlight from heaven. She looked around the room, saw her sweater folded neatly on the desk, draped it around her shoulders. Feeling the carpet on her bare feet, she found her slippers by the bed and slipped her feet into them. Quiet now. Her younger sister, Louisa, asleep in the other bed. She could see her now, the hump under the covers, the slow up and down of her breaths. Louisa, still young enough to tell their mother if she saw or heard. Quiet. Like a mouse.

The hall was bright and still. She would always take the stairs—couldn't risk the main halls, her father making his way back to his room, the last whiskey still in his hand, the anger if he ever found her sneaking out. The door was the same—heavy but quiet, the gray concrete stairs hard and certain. Down, down, out the side door, onto the brick walkway, the night cooler, but still warm, the moon a huge white orb against the black sky.

She stopped at the end of the building where the walkway split. For a moment she stood still, staring straight ahead, listening. The porch looked out over the ocean, and the distant slaps of the waves rolling onto the beach were faint but unmistakable. The ocean that the two of them would stare at from one of the wicker love-seats, or from the wooden steps, their arms around each other, Walker's hardness pushing against her thigh, almost begging for release. She remembered the unnerving strangeness of it, this live thing between them as the mosquitoes droned and dove around their heads. And then the fear would take over again, the fear of her father finding her in Walker's arms, and, blaming the incessant biting of the mosquitoes, she would sneak back to bed.

She followed the sound of the ocean, gentle in the night. She started to hurry. She knew he would leave if she got there too late, he afraid of his own father and the angry whiskey.

She came around a bend in the walkway and saw the ocean and the moonlight splayed out wide across the black of the sea. By feel now. By gray distant memory now. The porch, only yards from the edges of the hard sand.

The walkway turned. Lily didn't. That was not the way. Not to the porch and Walker.

She kept moving, feeling the walkway turn to hard earth through her slippers, then to grass. Cool grass moist with early dew, coating her slippers and ankles. Darker now, the huge cypress trees eating the moonlight. She pulled her sweater tightly around her shoulders and held it to her with her arms. A low-lying branch draped with moss raked her shoulder. She stopped, looking and listening for the waves. She couldn't hear them now, but she could smell water. She moved past the branch, into an opening from the trees. The grass was deeper here, thick and wet, the rough serrated blades brushing her legs like little saws, scratching her calves in long red thin lines.

And then it was dark again in front of her—a ribbon of dark as dark could be. Musty dark, watery dark, only a sliver of moonlight brushing its surface as if it were a water snake gliding toward its home.

And then she was sliding on the muddy incline, falling toward the ribbon of black winding its way through the canopy of trees. Slipping and falling, the musty ribbon of dark swallowing her whole as the gentle rolls of the sea curled and died on the hard sand just a hundred yards away.

Something woke Val shortly after dawn. It was partly her heart thumping against its bony cage, partly an innate and sudden unnerving sense of something gone terribly awry. Thump, thump, skip, thump, thump, thump, thump.

She blinked, blinked again, turned, saw the empty bed next to her. For a long moment, she shut her eyes and prayed to God for Lily.

"Lily," she yelled.

Nothing.

"Lily!"

Nothing.

Pressure now, her chest tightening, the aging, thumping muscle begging for air. She sat up, the room blurring from the sudden motion. She had to sit still for several seconds to let her head clear. Then up and to the bathroom. No Lily. Back out into the room. She looked at the desk. Lily's sweater that she had neatly folded the night before was gone. The slippers she had set next to Lily's bed were gone.

She almost tore her nightgown off, dressed as fast as she could, picked up all the room cards from the desk.

Walker's room was across the hall. She opened the door and stopped next to his bed. He was sound asleep, snoring, his mouth open. A half-empty cocktail glass was on the nightstand next to him, an empty pint of vodka on the floor.

She almost shook him awake but then decided it would take too much time to rouse him.

She was down and into the lobby in a minute. Thump, thump, skip, skip, thump. Police officer at the desk talking quietly with two managers. She walked out through the front doors and stopped as the doorman closed the doors behind her.

"Is everything okay?" she said.

"I'm not sure, ma'am." He looked toward the ocean. "One of the guests might have had an accident."

"Where? In the ocean?"

"I really can't say, ma'am. An ambulance did head that way." He nodded toward the lobby. "The manager's inside. He might know."

"Gosh, I hope they're okay," Val said, turning for the side walkway. As soon as she turned the corner, she began to run and then had to slow, her chest squeezing the air out of her. She passed a wing of the hotel, turned toward the ocean, saw the flashing lights several hundred yards away in the grove of cypress trees flanking the canal that bordered the property. She walked as fast as she could, holding her sweater over her shoulders tight to her.

Two Georgia State Police cars; one ambulance; two maintenance workers in golf carts; eight to ten other people standing around watching. The back doors of the ambulance were open with two paramedics standing by the door talking to two police officers.

Val came up to the group of people milling around. "Oh my, what happened?"

An elderly woman in walking clothes with her hand over her mouth turned toward her. "The workers found a woman in the canal this morning," she said. "She must have gotten lost. I think she was in her nightgown."

"Oh my God," Val said. "She's just hurt? Or she…she drowned?" The woman nodded.

"If the gators didn't get 'er," said a teenage boy in waiter's clothes straddling a bicycle. "There's a big-ass momma gator in there. Probably ten foot. They got 'er all covered up too. I was watching when they took 'er out and put 'er in the ambulance. I bet that gator got 'er."

Val took several steps toward the ambulance and then had to stop, the grass and trees spinning around her. Her stomach burned up into her throat and she was leaning over, retching, gasping, retching, gasping.

The elderly woman put a hand on her back. "Can I help you? Did you know her? They don't know who she is yet."

Val straightened and wiped her mouth. The paramedics were closing the back doors of the ambulance. She felt herself moving, stepping backward, shaking her head no, mouthing something to the woman.

She turned, walked a few yards, stopped. She wiped her mouth with her sweater and then her eyes and cheeks. She closed her eyes, took a deep breath, opened them.

Time to man up, Walker, she said to herself. Time to man up.

GOLDIE

"Wake up, Goldie. We need to go."

Goldie's eyes opened. She blinked several times and got up on her elbows. "Why? What happened?"

Val was opening Goldie's blinds, looking out into the courtyard, wiping her eyes.

"What happened, Val? What's the matter? You look awful."

"Lily got up during the night, and I guess she tried to walk to the porch. She got lost."

Val sat down on the edge of the bed and put her face in her hands.

"And what, Val? She's lost?"

"No, she's not lost." Val started to shake, slowly at first, then uncontrollably.

"What is it, Val? Just say it."

"She drowned, Goldie. She walked into the canal and drowned."

"Oh no. Oh my god, no." Goldie got up, moved next to Val, put her arms around her.

After several minutes Val stopped shaking. She wiped her eyes, put her face in her hands for a few more seconds, and then pushed herself up from the bed. We need to go, Goldie. I'm going to wake up Sophie and Walker."

"What do you mean, Val? We can't go. What about Lily? What about Walker?"

"She's dead, Goldie. There's nothing we can do for her. Walker's going to have to handle it."

"Walker's going to have to handle it? Are you serious? We're just going to take off and let Walker handle Julie and God knows what else?"

"Goldie, the police are already at the canal, and I expect that as soon as they figure out who Lily is, they're going to be knocking on my door. I'm leaving, and I'm pretty sure Sophie will be going with me. If you want to go to Florida anytime soon and see Rhonda, I would suggest that you come as well. If you don't want to, I understand. I'll fly you down there whenever you want."

Goldie put her face in her hands.

"I'm going to wake up Sophie and Walker. I really do understand if you want to stay. Meet me at the 'Bago if you want to come with us. And go down the stairs, please. There's too much going on in the lobby."

Sophie was asleep, a half-full glass of wine on the nightstand next to her bed. Val shook her until her eyes opened.

"You need to get up, Sophie. We need to leave."

Val pulled Sophie's suitcase out of the closet, opened it, put it on the bed. "I'll be back in five minutes."

"Five minutes? What's this, a New York funeral?"

"Five minutes," Val said sharply. "Unless you want to go home and see Roz, I need you out of here in five minutes. I'm serious."

Walker jerked awake when Val shook him. His eyes blinked rapidly and then focused on Val's face.

Val leaned over, put an arm around him, put her mouth right next to his ear. "Walker, I need you to listen to me. Are you awake? Do you hear me?"

Walker nodded.

"Your mother passed away this morning. She was a wonderful woman, and she loved you very much. I can't stay here for you now. I'll call Julie in a few minutes and tell her, but you're going to need to handle things here."

Walker was crying. Softly, silently.

"She loved you very much, Walker, and I know you loved her. You were a good son. Now you have to man up, Walker. I know you can."

Walker wiped his eyes and his nose.

"And you know what, Walker?"

Walker shook his head no.

Val kissed him on the cheek. "I love you, too." Val stood. "I'm leaving you plenty of money on the dresser, Walker. And when you talk to Julie, just tell her we're on our way home. She can always reach me on my phone."

Goldie fortunately had left her two large bags in the storage compartment of the 'Bago. She helped Sophie down the side stairs with her bags and then across the parking lot. Val already had the engine started. Sitting in the 'Bago, she'd watched another police car come down the main driveway followed by what she thought was a news van. She got out, helped them put the suitcase in, hurried them up the steps.

Sophie was quiet, her face drawn. "I don't like this, Val. It's not right."

"Of course it's not right. It's wrong. It's terrible. It's horrible. It's despicable. We can stay if you want. You can stay if you want. I'll fly you home today." Val put the 'Bago in drive but kept her foot on the brake.

Val wiped her eyes. "You don't think I loved Lily? You don't think I've spent a thousand hours with her in the last two years? You don't think this is killing me?"

Silence.

"Look, Sophie, it's horrible. I know that. I also know I'm not ready to go home. I needed to get away, and I need more time. Walker will be okay, and you know Julie is going to be here on the first flight she can get. I can't deal with her now. I'm serious—you can stay and then go home. I'm sure Roz would love to see you. And, Goldie, whatever you want to do is fine." Val looked up at the main driveway. "I'm leaving, though. I really don't feel like spending the morning with the Georgia State Police."

"Well, I'm not going home," Sophie said. "I just want to say good-bye to Lily."

"I'm sure there will be a funeral in a few days. We can go home for that if we want."

"You know we're not going home for that," Sophie said, wiping her eyes.

"We'll have our own service then. That would be better anyway." Val looked to Goldie.

"Don't look at me—I'm going to Florida."

Val put on her sunglasses, took her foot off the brake, eased forward. Passing the circle to the front entrance of the Sea Grass, she shielded her face and looked straight ahead. Another news van passed them in the driveway. Val made it to the front road, turned, sped up.

"Now what?" Goldie asked.

Val's phone rang—a number with a Georgia area code. She let the call go to voice mail, put her hand in her purse, pulled out her iPad, handed it to Goldie. "We need to get rid of this thing. The RV website is bookmarked. See if there's a dealer in Jacksonville."

"Who's calling?" Sophie asked.

Val shrugged. "No one we want to talk to." She turned on her Bluetooth, picked up her phone, tapped on Julie's number. "You two don't have to listen to this if you don't want to. It's not going to be pretty."

Val stayed away from Interstate 95 and headed toward Jacksonville, Florida, on secondary roads. After Goldie had spoken with the Eastern RV Enterprises representative and then reserved a luxury sedan at a Hertz rental down the street, she handed Goldie her phone, the pad of paper, and a pen.

"I think I have a few messages," she said.

Goldie looked at the phone. "A few?"

"See if there's anything from Walker first. I want to make sure he's okay."

Goldie scrolled through Val's texts, phone calls, voice messages, and e-mails. "Nothing from Walker. The usuals, plus this person from Georgia has called three times, and there are two other calls from a different number in Georgia."

"Maybe do Georgia first then."

"You want me to put it on speaker?"

"No. I don't want to hear it."

Goldie put the cord microphone in her ear, adjusted the notepad on her lap, tapped on the phone, started writing. Five minutes later, she took the earpiece out, pursed her lips, turned in her seat to face Val.

Val turned back onto Route 17 toward Jacksonville. "I'm listening."

"I'll start with the good news first." She turned a little more in her seat so Sophie could hear her. "Mo is still doing well after her surgery. She'll be in the hospital for a few more days and then in rehab for a little while, but Mary Catherine expects she'll be able to go home." Looking back to Val, she said, "And she's waiting for a call from you. Mary Catherine that is."

Goldie turned to face Sophie for a moment. "Roz is going berserk. She says she's called you a hundred times, and you won't answer. Val, she says she's called you two hundred times, and she's close to calling the police to find you."

"I'm on vacation," Sophie said. "I don't look at my phone. I don't even know where it is."

"Well, you might want to find it and call her today."

"And Georgia?"

"I'm getting to that. The same for you with Bill, Val. He's getting a little agitated. Maybe a lot agitated. Debbie called, too. She sounded okay, but you should call her when you get a chance."

Val nodded. "I will. What's with the Georgia numbers?"

"Sergeant Cook from the Georgia State Police wants to speak with you. Today, he said. And Detective Callahan from the Macomb County Sheriff's Department also wants to know where you are. Apparently Julie has filed some kind of order to find you." Goldie's phone chimed, and she paused to glance at it.

"And?" Val said.

Goldie tapped out a text message on her own phone. "And the general manager of the Sea Grass wants to speak with you as soon as possible." She looked up and paused. "Apparently Walker isn't making a whole lot of sense."

Val nodded and shrugged. "As I said, we need to get rid of this thing."

Val drove to the Hertz rental first. She rented a luxury Lincoln sedan for two weeks with a return in Bethesda, Maryland. Goldie already had the bags out of the 'Bago by the time she got back out to the parking lot, and she was now carrying out a box of wine bottles. Val opened the trunk and started putting the bags in. Goldie went back one last time and carried out the last of the wine and a bag of snacks.

Val walked through the 'Bago and checked all the compartments, the closets, the bathroom. "Ready?" she said from the door.

Goldie nodded. Sophie just stared at her and shook her head sideways.

"The keys are on the front seat. Why don't you wait for me at that McDonald's across the street? I can walk that far. I don't want them to see the car."

"Gotcha. You want anything to eat or drink."

"No thanks. You two get something. See you in a few."

Val paid for the 'Bago in cash, declined a receipt, and, stopping every hundred yards to catch her breath, finally made it over to the McDonald's where Goldie and Sophie were drinking coffee and eating Egg McMuffins.

"So how long will it take to get to Naples?" Sophie asked Val between bites.

"About six hours," Goldie said, looking at her phone.

Sophie looked to Val and then back to Goldie. "You do a lot of traveling with Rhonda, huh?"

Goldie shrugged. "Not so much. We go to Amelia Island sometimes. It's pretty close to here, so I know the drive."

Sophie looked at Val again; Val shook her head no.

Sophie took another bite, chewed, set her Egg McMuffin down. "So, Val, what are we going to do while Vicky has her playdate?"

Val was typing on her phone. "I'm making a reservation at the Ritz. Is that okay?"

"It'll do. Have you been there, Vicky? Is it nice?"

"Which one? There's one on the beach and one off Airport Road inland."

"The one on the Gulf," Val said.

"It's beautiful. There's a great pool and a really cute tiki bar."

Sophie shot Val another look and rolled her eyes. "Are we going to get to meet Rhonda this time, or are you going to keep her all to yourself?"

"I think she has plans for us tonight, but sure. I really do want you to meet her. I've told her so much about you all that she feels like she knows you. Maybe we can do something tomorrow."

"Special night tonight?" Sophie asked, wiping her mouth with a napkin.

Goldie looked up from her phone. "They're all special, Sophie."

Bill called when they were two hours north of Naples on I-75. Val let it go to voice mail and then listened to it herself: "Mom, you need to call me right away."

Val drove a few more miles before she called him back.

"Hi, Bill. You sound worried. Is there something wrong?"

"I don't know, maybe you should tell me. I thought you were in Atlantic City."

Val looked at Goldie, who shrugged and lifted her hands. "We were. We decided to leave. Is something wrong?"

"Mom, some guy from Hertz just called me about the car you rented in my name in Jacksonville, Florida. You got the insurance number wrong."

"Oh," Val said after a moment. "I'm sorry. I was going to tell you about the car. A bunch of lights keep coming on in my car. There's a Lexus dealer there that's going to work on it."

Val looked to Goldie again and shrugged her shoulders.

"And you gave them a wrong phone number for me. It took them a while to get the right William Kantor."

"My bad. Sorry. See what happens when you get old."

"You have all of my numbers in your phone."

Silence.

"When did you go to Florida? You just told me the other day you were in Atlantic City."

"The next day I guess. We were getting bored. And losing too much money."

Silence.

"Bored? Right. You've never been bored." Pause. "You drove to Florida in one day? That's a bit much, isn't it?"

"It wasn't too bad. Goldie drove part of the way."

"So, I don't understand. They said you were returning the car back here. Are you coming home, or are you staying there until they fix your car?"

"We're sort of on our way home. It might take a few days, though. We're going to take our time on the way back."

"And what about your car, Mom?"

"I'll either fly back down, or they said I could pay someone to drive it back up."

"So you're tooling around Florida in a rental car."

"It's a Lincoln. It's fine. It's rather nice, actually. I might trade my Lexus in and get one of these. Honey, I'm sorry, I'll call you back in a little bit. I have another call."

"Mom—"

Val ended the call and stared at the highway ahead. "I knew that Hertz guy was a moron," she said.

Her phone lit up again: Eastern RV Enterprises.

"Yes?"

"Is this Mrs. Kantor?"

"Yes."

"We just wanted to let you know what was going on."

"I'm listening."

"We've gotten some calls about your 'Bago rental this afternoon from the Georgia State Police and the Macomb County Sheriff's Office. Our policy is not to give out any information without your permission, so we didn't, but if they get a warrant or a subpoena, then we have to."

"I understand. That's fine. I appreciate the call. And I know what it's about, so even if they do call back, it's no big deal."

"Okay. We just wanted to let you know."

"Christ, what's next?" Val said, ending the call. She looked in the rearview mirror at Sophie sleeping in the back seat. "Did she ever call Roz today? It's been so busy I forgot to ask."

"Yeah, I got caught up talking to Rhonda and forgot to tell you. She called her from McDonald's. It didn't go so well."

"No? Why, what happened?"

"I don't really know all of it. I could hear Roz getting loud, and Sophie just hung up on her."

"Great." Val checked the lanes behind her with her mirrors and sped up. "We need to get to Naples."

She passed a car, then another.

"We don't have to be there in ten minutes, Val," Goldie said. "Are you all right? You look a little pale."

Val eased back into the right lane. "Can you reach my purse?"

"Sure. What do you need?"

"I forgot to take one of my pills. I can get it, thanks." Val reached into her purse, unsnapped the bottle of nitroglycerin tablets with one hand, slipped one under her tongue.

Thump, skip, thump, thump, thump.

Rhonda lived in a gated golf course community close to downtown Naples. Goldie gave the guard at the gate her name and told him she was on the permanent guest list. He disappeared inside the guard house, reappeared a moment later, opened the gate, waved them in.

"Wow," Sophie said. "I'd come visit Rhonda, too. This is sweet in here."

"It's pretty nice," Goldie said. "Go left at the stop sign, Val, then right."

"Let me see," Sophie said, putting out her palms and moving them up and down. "Move in with David and Rachel, or move to paradise with Rhonda. Hmmm. Tough choice."

"I'm thinking about it," Goldie said.

"Yeah, I guess so."

"It's that house on the right, Val."

Val slowed, then turned into the circular driveway, around the fountain and the manicured lawn, and stopped in front of the large beige stucco house.

"Holy Moly," Sophie said. "Where'd she get all her dough?"

"Nice house," Val said.

"You can just drop me here," Goldie said. "I don't think she's home. I have a key."

"Are you sure? We can wait here with you."

"No, it's fine. Who knows when she'll be home. You two go get checked into your hotel. You'll love it."

Val got out, opened the trunk, helped Goldie get her suitcases and garment bags up to the tile porch fronting the mahogany door.

"Have fun, Vicky," Sophie said through the open car window.

"I'll text you or call you in a little while," Goldie said. "If we don't see you tonight, we'll have lunch or something tomorrow."

Val hugged her and then hugged her again. "Say hi to Rhonda," she said.

⟞⟝

Goldie actually did text Val two hours later: u want to have a drink at the bar there?

Val: sure, the tiki bar?

Goldie: yes, half an hour?

Val: sure, c u then

Sophie was sitting out on the balcony with a glass of wine watching the sun go down. Val poured herself a glass and sat down next to her.

"Goldie's coming over with Rhonda for a drink in a half-hour," she said. "We're going to meet them in the tiki bar."

"Really."

"That's what she said."

"Hmm. I have to admit that I was not expecting that tonight."

"Nor was I. She's just full of surprises, isn't she?"

"Yes she is. She certainly is."

⟞⟝

Goldie walked into the tiki bar of the Naples Ritz Carlton holding onto "Rhonda's" arm. Goldie was in her new jeans, a new orange top, and smiling. She said something to Rhonda and looked around the bar. Rhonda looked to be somewhere around Goldie's age. Rhonda was six feet tall, slim, handsome, tan. Rhonda was wearing shorts, loafers, and a golf shirt open at the neck with a gold chain showing on his chest. Goldie saw them and spoke in his ear. Beaming, she waved and guided him around the tables.

"Val, Sophie, this is my friend Saul."

"I knew I needed to meet this Rhonda," Sophie said. "You got any friends?"

"Stop it, Sophie," Val said, extending her hand. "Hi, I'm Val. It's so nice to meet you."

"My pleasure. And you must be Sophie." Saul let go of Val's hand and reached to Sophie.

Goldie's right arm was still hooked around Saul's left arm, with her left hand now resting on her right. Sophie was looking at her hand when she reached out to shake Saul's. "Yeah, I'm Sophie. I'm the obnoxious one."

"Oh, Sophie, you know I would never say that," Goldie said. "You're the funny one."

"Yeah, I'm hilarious. Just ask Roz." Sophie let go of Saul's hand and looked back to Goldie's. "Is that a new ring, Vicky?"

Goldie looked at her left ring finger, squeezed Saul's arm, smiled. "Yes, it is. Saul just gave it to me. Isn't it beautiful?"

SOPHIE

"Well, I'm just glad we didn't have to call her out on it," Sophie said, a piece of syrup-drenched Belgium waffle poised near her mouth. "I was damn close, I can tell you that."

Val took a sip of coffee and looked out to the Gulf of Mexico. "She's too good of a friend to never tell us at all," she finally said. "Maybe she didn't really know herself until now. Maybe she was just being honest in her own way."

"Oh, bullshit. She's not Vicky because she shops at Penny's."

"True. But this is a lot more than just having fun. And her family's going to flip out. You know that."

"Well, they're stupid then. What did they think she was doing in Florida on all those trips? Or maybe I should say *who* did they think she was doing."

"Visiting Rhonda. Like we did."

"Not me. I knew why she was shopping at Vicky's." Sophie speared a piece of waffle and held it up to the light. "I mean, this Rhonda was supposed to be her best friend. Had they ever met her? Had we ever met her? For heaven's sake, is there even a Rhonda at all?"

"That's a good question. I tend to think not. But I don't think that has ever crossed their minds. All they saw was her taking care of Frank."

"As I said then, they're stupid. I don't think there is a Rhonda. And Frank may as well have been dead for a long time. I mean, that's why you killed him, isn't it?"

Val's coffee cup was on her lips. She jerked, the cup tilting and spilling a stream of brown onto the white tablecloth.

"Christ," Sophie went on, "for all I know you've known about this Saul guy the whole time. Maybe she asked you to do it. Maybe I'm the dumb one here."

"I'm sorry. What did you say?"

Sophie looked around at the other tables on the outdoor patio and leaned closer to Val. "I said that maybe that's why you killed him. Because he was basically dead anyway, and maybe, just maybe, you wanted to free her up for this Saul guy."

Val looked around herself, squinted, hardened her voice. "I really hope I'm not hearing what I think I'm hearing from you. Particularly about Goldie. How could you ever say that?" Val wiped the tablecloth with her napkin and leaned closer. "And why would I want to 'kill' Frank, as you say?"

Sophie took a bite of waffle, chewed it, leaned over again so that her face was only a foot from Val's. "Because you couldn't stand the fact that he was a gork, and he was eating up all her money," she said softly. "And you, in your infinite wisdom, were going to help her whether she wanted it or not."

"You really are insane. And just how would I go about killing Frank, sweetness?"

"Oh, don't sweetness me now. You're the sweet one who did it."

Val just stared at her.

Sophie leaned back, took another bite, leaned over again. "If I were a detective, I would say you put enough Valium down his feeding tube to stop a horse from breathing."

"Oh, is that right. 'Down his feeding tube.' And why would you think that?"

"Because you were there when he died. And first you said he had a stroke. And then you said he just stopped breathing." Sophie leaned back and wiped her mouth with her napkin. "And then you said, 'What difference does it make? Dead is dead.'"

Val leaned back and looked into her coffee cup for a moment. Then, opening her purse, she put some cash on the table and stood. "You've got a lot of nerve, sweetness."

"I'm just saying, Val. You don't have to get so huffy about it. Goldie's obviously happy."

Val took a couple of steps away, turned, looked back at Sophie.

Sophie put up her hand. "Just tell me, Val. I'd really like to know."

"Tell you what? That I killed Frank? I didn't kill Frank. Frank was already dead as you say."

"No. I don't really care whether you killed Frank or you didn't kill Frank. But I do care whether Goldie had anything to do with it. I'd like to know if the two of you have been lying to me the whole time. I'd like to know if I should be happy for her or whether she could be one of the biggest bitches in the world and I just never saw it."

"Oh, and what would that make me?"

Sophie cocked her head and squinted at Val. "Well, it wouldn't make you sweetness, would it?"

Val stared at her a moment longer. "Happy, Sophie. Maybe just for once in your life. Happy."

"Where are you going?"

"Happy, Sophie. Not for you. For Goldie. For your friend. Before you don't have any more."

"Val—"

Val put up a hand and kept moving.

"Val—"

≈‡ ‡≈

Sophie went to the porch railing and watched Val make her way around the pool and out toward the walkway to the beach. She stopped twice along the way, apparently to catch her breath. Once she opened her purse, took something out, put it in her mouth. Sophie watched her go down the walkway, watched her pause at the steps down to the beach, watched her make her way down the steps, and then take her shoes off when she reached the sand. She watched Val tread gingerly over the sand, pause, tread, pause. She watched her make it to the edge of the Gulf, roll her pants up, walk into the water ankle high. Then she turned and headed toward the lobby and the elevators.

Whoosh, whoosh, whoosh. Three cups of coffee had not dented the throbbing deep in her head. Whoosh, whoosh! Her vision clouded, and she stopped. She put her hand on the wall and waited until it cleared. Then she moved off again, slowly now, the pounding still there but better when she moved gently, quietly.

The lobby was busy with well-dressed guests in business attire, golf attire, and upscale outer swimwear. Sophie made her way over the marble floors, past the central atrium, past the front desk. In the elevator on the way to the fifth floor, she took out her hotel key cards—one for her room and one for Val's room. The night before, deciding that one of them might need the other, they had swapped cards before they went to bed.

Open Val's door. Whoosh. Val's suitcase was out and open on the unused bed. Whoosh, whoosh. She moved Val's clothes around, took some out, put them back. She looked around the room, saw a pill bottle on the nightstand, walked over to it—nitroglycerin 0.4 mg tablets. Whoosh. She made her way to the bathroom. Lavender-embroidered makeup bag was on the vanity, white-cloth toiletry bag next to it. She looked around, opened the cabinet below the sink—black-cloth zippered bag. She opened it, didn't bother to read the labels on the plastic sandwich bags. She already knew what they said. She took all of them and put them in her purse. Whoosh, whoosh, *whoosh*!

Black bag back under the sink. Pause once more at the toiletry bag, take out Val's plastic daily pill container. Study it for a moment. There were no empty little spaces—both rows, a.m. and p.m., were full of pills.

Out in the bedroom. Now what? Her cell phone was ringing—ignore it.

Back to the bathroom. Spill Val's bags out onto the marble counter. Back to the bedroom. Toss clothes from the suitcase over the bed and on the floor. Open several dresser drawers and leave them open.

Whoosh, whoosh, *whoosh!*

Back to her room, head throbbing, vision clouding again. Pause until she could see. Go to the bathroom, get all of her pill bottles. Go to the closet, open the safe. Bottles and sandwich bags in the safe. Lock it.

Lie down on her bed. Cell phone ringing, again and again.

Whoosh, whoosh, *whoosh!*

⚞⚟

She woke to a pounding on the door, and then her name being called. She sat, the room spinning. Pound, pound. Spin, spin. Finally the spinning stopped.

"Hold your horses!" she said as loud as she could. She went to the door—Goldie.

"Oh my God, you're here. I've been calling you and calling you. And neither of you are even registered here. Wait until Bill hears about this one."

Sophie rubbed her eyes. "What's the matter, Vicky? Did Rhonda kick you out already?"

"Val's in the hospital, Sophie. We need to get into her room and get her medications. They don't know what she's on. Maybe the front desk will let you in."

"The hospital? I was just—" Sophie looked at her watch. "I guess I fell asleep. That was a couple of hours ago. What happened?'

"I don't know. All I know is they called me from the emergency room and wanted to know what medicines she's on. That's how I got your room number."

"Okay," Sophie said, rubbing her eyes. "I have a key. Let me get my purse."

"Oh, thank God. Come on, let's go."

Sophie opened Val's door, walked in, stopped. "Holy Moly. Someone must have broken in here. Val would never leave her room like this."

Goldie looked around. "I hope that's not what happened to her."

"I know she keeps her medications in her bathroom bag," Sophie said, heading toward the bathroom. "And there's a bottle over there on the nightstand. Why don't you grab that one?"

Five minutes later they walked out the front door of the Ritz Carlton. "We'll have to come back later and tell them that someone broke into her room," Goldie said. "We don't have time now."

A bellman waved to a valet parker who saw Goldie and went to a black Mercedes convertible that was pulled over in the driveway. He sped it around the circle and opened the doors for them.

"Nice ride," Sophie said. "Rhonda's, I presume? Or do you have your own now?"

Goldie sped out without answering. "When was the last time you saw her?"

"We had breakfast, and then she wanted to go walking on the beach. I went up to my room. They didn't tell you anything when they called you?"

"No. They weren't very helpful on the phone. I wonder if she had a problem on the beach. Sometimes it's hard walking on that sand. And I think she's having more problems with her heart then she lets on."

"Maybe. I've been thinking she's been short of breath lately. And having a bottle of nitroglycerin by your bed probably isn't the best sign." Sophie looked at the pill container they had taken from the bathroom. "She's not always so good about taking her medications either. This is full."

"No surprise. She's always so worried about taking care of us that she doesn't take of herself."

"That's true. Very true."

Goldie sped through a yellow light and turned onto Immokalee Road. "It's right up here. I think it's supposed to be a pretty good hospital."

"I'm sure they get a lot of practice down here," Sophie said. "It's probably a good place to get sick."

With some badgering and mild threats of malpractice suits and personal attorneys, Goldie and Sophie were fairly quickly let back into the emergency room and then into one of the cardiac bays. Val was in a hospital gown reclining on a gurney. A doctor in scrubs and a white coat was on one side of her, and a man in a coat and tie holding a clipboard was on the other. As soon as Val saw them, she rolled her eyes and looked at the doctor.

"You see, my friends are here. I'm fine. I really do appreciate your help."

The doctor looked at Goldie and Sophie and shook his head. "No, you're not fine, but I'm not going to argue with you anymore."

"Are you okay, honey?" Goldie said, moving to her side. "Oh my gosh, we've been so worried. What happened?"

"I'm fine," Val said. "I just forgot to take my medicines this morning."

Sophie looked at her and raised her eyebrows but stayed quiet.

"Her heart rate is very high, her blood pressure is high, and she has an arrhythmia," the doctor said. "And she thinks she's fine."

"And she wants to sign out AMA," said the man on the other side of the bed. "Against medical advice."

"Oh, honey, maybe you should stay here for a little while," Goldie said. "Something must have happened."

"Yeah, it did. I was resting on the beach, and some doctor was walking by and thought I looked ill. Then he took my pulse and got all hyper about it. My heart rate is always high." She looked at the ER doctor. "Call my doctor at home if you want—he'll tell you."

"I'm not sure 'resting' is the right word, Mrs. Kantor," the doctor said. "He said you were wheezing and having trouble breathing, and you weren't responding."

"I was thinking about my friend who just died."

The doctor just looked at her.

"Well, I do appreciate his opinion and his help," Val said. "Don't get me wrong. But I know myself, and all I need are my pills, and I'll be fine." She reached for the clipboard that the hospital administrator was holding. "May I use your pen please?"

The doctor shrugged. "Okay, but I just need to tell you a few things so that you clearly understand before you sign that. We are advising you to be admitted to the hospital and have a full cardiac evaluation for a possible myocardial infarction or some other cardiac or pulmonary problem. Do you understand?"

Val nodded and signed the paper.

"We'll be here if you need help. We gave you a beta-blocker, so your rate is down, but it will wear off pretty quickly. I would strongly suggest you get back on your medications pronto."

"We brought them, honey," Goldie said. "Are you sure you want to do this?"

"I'm fine, Goldie. Really, I am. The morning was just a little stressful."

"We'll deal with your room later then," Goldie said. "I'll help you clean up."

"Why? What happened to my room?"

"Someone broke in and threw your stuff all around," Goldie said. "It's a good thing you had your purse with you."

Val looked at Sophie, pursed her lips, nodded slowly. "Is that right," she said. "Imagine that. In a Ritz Carlton even."

━⁺━ ━⁺━

"Do you feel any better?" Goldie asked when they were sitting down in the main dining room of the Naples Ritz Carlton. "You still look a little pale to me. Did you get back on all your medications?"

"I'm fine. I took a little nap. Thanks for cleaning up. That was quite a mess."

"It was. It's a little scary to tell you the truth. It's a good thing all of your good jewelry is at home."

"I always put it in my safety deposit box when I travel. You never know. Sophie, I'm surprised they didn't go in your room since you're right next to me."

"Maybe they did. My room is such a mess you couldn't tell."

"Well, thank God you weren't there," Goldie said.

Sophie reached in her purse, took out a bottle of Tylenol, took two dry. "Sorry," she said. "I've had a headache all day." Whoosh, whoosh.

"Don't be sorry, honey," Goldie said. "Are you okay? Do you want me to take you to a doctor?"

"No, I'll be fine."

Goldie looked at Saul. "Sophie has an aneurysm that she has to have surgery for when she gets home. I might go back for a few days when she has it done."

"I'm so sorry," Saul said. "That's tough surgery. Do you have family there? I can come up too if you need help."

"Oh, yeah. I've got plenty of family. Just check my phone. But that's very nice of you. Thank you."

"Well, Sophie, we're just a pair, aren't we?" Val said. "If we keep getting sick, these two aren't going to want to hang out with us."

"Oh, stop it," Goldie said, putting her hand on Saul's. "I am so happy you're here, and we can be together. I still feel so horrible about Mo. And it's been so busy here today I haven't even had much time to really think about Lily. Have you talked to Julie today?"

Val shook her head no. "They were talking about her in the emergency room. It was horrible. I wanted to cry."

Saul nodded solemnly. "It's been on the news a fair amount. It's so sad."

"Well, we'll have our own little service for her," Goldie said. "And for Mo, too." Goldie squeezed Saul's hand and looked up at him. "Maybe you should come up. I want you to meet Mo. She's the greatest. Right, Sophie? Isn't she the greatest?"

Sophie looked into her wine glass for a moment. "She really is, isn't she. Not a bad bone in her."

"Saul, you should have seen them playing cards. They're so funny together. Oh, my word. I can't even imagine what Las Vegas would have been like."

Sophie opened her purse and rummaged around in it. Looking up, she said, "I'm sorry to be a party pooper, but I don't feel so hot. I think I'm going to go up to my room. Val, I must have left my room key up there. May I use yours, please?"

Val looked at her for a moment before she opened her purse.

"You need to rest and get some sleep, honey," Goldie said. "Do you have anything to help you sleep?"

Val handed her the room key. "Do you have a Lunesta or something, Sophie? I'd give you one but whoever broke in took them all."

"I'll be fine. I just need to lie down." Sophie took the key and stood.

"I'll walk you up," Saul said.

"Thank you, but I'm fine. I'll see you tomorrow, I hope."

Goldie stood and hugged her. "Get some rest, dear."

Val looked at her, stood, moved around the table. "Come here, sweetness. Please."

Sophie moved around the table and met Val halfway.

Val took her in her arms, kissed her cheek, wiped the tear off it. "I love you, sweetness."

"I love you too, Val. I'm going to go lie down now."

"I know, honey. I love you."

VAL

Jules's big golden head is radiant in the morning sun. In the chair next to you, he's gazing out at the water, at the infinite blue of it, at the specks of white raised by the soft breeze and the larger frothings of the birds diving and plucking their breakfast from the sea. You reach for him, put your hand on his muscular arm, run it down his forearm. You take his hand and intertwine his fingers in yours, the rising sun warm on your backs, the gentle edges of the water brushing your feet, then rolling back to the mother force.

You stir in your bed, your arm wrapped around the pillow beside you. Thump, thump, thump. Louder and louder, faster and faster, the dying ball of muscle crying out for air. No! you scream at it. Not now! Leave me alone! Leave him alone!

And somehow this day, for some unknown reason, it obeys you. It flips in its bony bed one more time, and then, as if it itself were tired of its own antics, it calms, slows.

You take your other hand and put it over his, feeling the roughness of his knuckles, the skin over his bones. The sun rises a little farther and the children come in on a small wave, their heads out of the water like little ducks cruising toward the shore. They stay there in the shallows of the sea, laughing as the water rolls over them and out, over them and out. They are young, Bill twelve or so, Debbie maybe six, Roger four. Too young to know what lies ahead of them. Too young to know anything but the water and the sun and the laughter.

Thump, thump, skip, skip, thump. Refreshed from its respite, the animal is wild again, and there is no denying it now. You wake, gasping for air. You raise yourself on your pillow, instinctively reach for the bottle next to the bed, then move your hand away from it. You close your eyes and force yourself calm. Slow, deep breaths. Calm. You have to say calm.

Jules is gone. No bringing him back now. Not with the animal in your chest writhing as if it were trapped, as if it were the one who wanted to be free. Not with your phone ringing yet again. Almost incessantly now, the calls one after the other: Georgia, Julie, Roz, Bill, Mary Catherine, Goldie, Georgia, Georgia, Julie, Roz, Julie.

You look at your phone—twenty-two missed calls, twelve unanswered voice messages.

You go into the bathroom, brush your teeth, brush your hair. You study your face in the mirror—gray and drawn. No matter.

You go out to the writing desk in the room and sit down. Calm, catch your breath. You need to talk. You call Scott Yureman's office, hoping he's not yet in his office. It is, after all, not even 8:00 a.m. yet.

Scott's recorded voice comes through, a lengthy message saying not to leave trading orders on the phone as they could not be executed via voice mail. You wait for the message to end, and then you take a breath.

"Scott, this is Val. I'm still away, and I'm not sure when I'll be back. Maybe in a few days, but I'm not sure." You pause to take another breath. "And just in case I'm not back soon, I need you to listen to me carefully, Scott. I want you to open that envelope I gave you. There's a key to my safety deposit box in it. I want you to go to my bank and open my box—you're on the list, so don't worry about that." Pause, breathe, breathe. "There's a new will in the box. You and Bill are now co-executors of my estate. The instructions in my will are clear, particularly about whatever money is left. The jewelry in the box is for my granddaughters. There are instructions in the will for that as well. Take care, Scott. And thank you. You're a good man."

Thump, skip, thump, thump, thump! Faster now, harder now.

You pull the drapes open. The sun is coming up over the front of the hotel erasing the shadows over the pool and patios in the back. You put on shorts, a top, a sweater, sandals. You put your phone in silent mode and put it in your purse.

You go down to the hotel desk, slowly, stopping every ten yards or so to catch your breath. You explain the lost keys to the Ritz trainee and get new keys. Back upstairs, even slower now, chest pounding and pounding.

You open Sophie's door. The room is quiet but for the humming of the air conditioner. The room is deathly quiet. Oh, you say to yourself, don't start that now. Don't start crying now. *You* let her take them. You! You *knew* what was she was doing. *You* gave her the room key.

You take a deep breath, then another. You walk into her bedroom, the tears flowing now. Sophie on the bed, her eyes closed, her face peaceful. You kiss her cheek, pull the covers over her. You wipe the tears away and kiss her again. You pick up all the bags and empty pill bottles and put them in your purse. You kiss her one last time.

Out into the hall now, down to the elevator, down to the patios. Walk, stop, walk, stop. You sit in a chair by the pool and take out your phone. You text Roz: Sophie passed away in her sleep last night. Peacefully, thank God. You need to come down here. Ritz

Carlton on the Gulf in Naples, Florida. Rm 515. If I'm not there, I'll be on the beach. Then you text Goldie: Please come over in a while. I need u. Luv u, honey.

Slowly, oh so slowly now, you go to the walkway and down the steps. The beach attendant is waiting for you.

"Are you okay, ma'am? Do you need help?'

You catch your breath. "Yes, please. Would you please take a chair down to the water for me?" You take out a hundred dollar bill and hand it to him. "And if you don't mind, would you bring one down for my husband, too? Thank you so much."

You take your sandals off, the sand still cool from the night. You take a step. The sand is gritty, hard, cool. You go a few yards, stop, go a few more yards, stop. The attendant already has one chair at the edge of the water and is headed back for the other.

"Are you okay, ma'am? I'll help you down to the water if you want."

"I'm fine, thank you. I'm just taking it easy on my knees with this sand."

"Okay, well, just let me know."

Ten more yards. Stop, rest. You make it to the chair, hold onto the back of it, catch your breath.

"Is that where you want it? I can move it if you want."

"Would you move them both a little closer to the water please? We like to feel the waves."

"Sure. You want this one right next to yours?"

"Yes, please. As close as you can get it."

"There you go. Let me know if you need anything."

"Okay. Thank you." Deep breath. Calm now. "Thank you so much."

You sit in the chair. The sun is higher now, almost hot on your back, but the water is cool, slipping over your feet and letting loose the tiny granules of sand that work their way between your toes.

You close your eyes. The breeze is soft and gentle on your cheek. You pull your sweater around your arms. The voices around you soften and recede into the sounds of the water and the birds.

You see Henry first. Henry, of all people. Bill's father. Pretty much all that is left of those years so long ago. Henry, bent in the escape of his garden, his knees in the grass, his hands working their way through the flower bed. Henry, sad and crying when you'd left him, you too strong, him too weak.

Then you see your children again. Roger, Debbie, Bill. One after the other. Forward, backward, their faces large and filling your mind, then dim and fading.

Thump, skip, thump! Thump! Thump! Thump! The animal in your chest is crazed! You can feel it flipping and writhing and gasping for air. There's not much time, you think. No time at all, you think. The time, it went so fast, you think.

You reach out and put your hand on Jules's arm. You squeeze it, telling him it's time. He turns, his eyes piercing discs of sapphire in the reflections of the blue sea. He smiles at you. He leans close to kiss you and rub his stubbly cheek over yours. He touches your chest and runs his finger between your breasts. He stands, takes your hand, lifts you out of the chair. He leads you into the water, shallow at first, then deeper, cooler. He takes your shoulders and pulls you to him. He pulls you close to him, as close as you can possibly go. He pulls you so close that you are one with him. You are one with him forever in the deep blue sea.

Thump...thump..........thump... . . . .

THE END

ABOUT THE AUTHOR

John O'Neill graduated from the College of William and Mary and received his medical degree from the Georgetown University School of Medicine. He is a medical practitioner in the Washington, DC, area and has been named one of DC's top doctors by the *Washingtonian* magazine and other publications.

O'Neill used his medical expertise to write the medical thrillers *Baby Girl Lauren* and *Blue Death*. His latest book, *The 'Bago Blues*, focuses on the patients' journey instead of the doctors'.

www.ingramcontent.com/pod-product-compliance
Lightning Source LLC
Chambersburg PA
CBHW060137130626
46556CB00006B/2380